spin with me

spin with me

AMI POLONSKY

Farrar Straus Giroux Books for Young Readers
An imprint of Macmillan Children's Publishing Group, LLC
120 Broadway, New York, NY 10271

Printed in the United States of America by LSC Communications,
Harrisonburg, Virginia
Designed by Cassie Gonzales
First edition, 2021
1 3 5 7 9 10 8 6 4 2

mackids.com

Library of Congress Cataloging-in-Publication Data
Names: Polonsky, Ami, author.
Title: Spin with me / Ami Polonsky.
Description: First edition. | New York : Farrar Straus Giroux Books for
    Young Readers, 2021. | Audience: Ages 8–12. | Audience: Grades 4–6. |
    Summary: Told in two voices, seventh-graders Essie, in North Carolina
    for just one semester, and Ollie, a nonbinary, "gender weird"
    classmate, develop a gentle romance while Essie ponders her label.
Identifiers: LCCN 2020007735 | ISBN 9780374313500 (hardcover)
Subjects: CYAC: Gender-nonconforming people—Fiction. |
    Friendship—Fiction. | Middle schools—Fiction. | Schools—Fiction.
Classification: LCC PZ7.P7687 Spi 2020 | DDC [Fic]—dc23
LC record available at https://lccn.loc.gov/2020007735

Our books may be purchased in bulk for promotional, educational, or
business use. Please contact your local bookseller or the Macmillan
Corporate and Premium Sales Department at (800) 221-7945 ext. 5442 or
by email at MacmillanSpecialMarkets@macmillan.com

For B & E again (because everything always),
but this time, especially for E

spin with
me

PART 1

BUTTERFLY

110 DAYS LEFT

"That's not exactly what I had in mind when I said you could decorate your bedroom however you wanted," Dad said from the doorway.

"It's just a line," I replied, standing on my bed, Sharpie in hand, as late afternoon sun slanted through the window.

"And tomorrow it will be two?"

"And then three . . . And it'll go all the way up to one hundred ten. Then we'll paint it over, go back home, and pretend this semester never happened."

He sighed his professorial sigh, adjusting his glasses. "Are you trying to tell me this quaint month-to-month rental is the proverbial prison?" Dad was a walking stereotype of a college professor: myopic, balding, lactose intolerant. And it was going to be the two of us, alone together, for exactly one hundred and ten days in a new city, in a new state, at a new school, for my first semester of seventh grade. All of this while life went on without me, back home.

"Come on, Esther," he continued. "You said today wasn't *totally* awful."

"It wasn't," I sighed, jumping down. The first day of school (the classic half day) had been fine. Mostly because it had ended at eleven thirty. *Before* lunch.

"Did you meet Ollie?" he prodded. Apparently someone Dad worked with had a kid in my grade. *Marianne told me Ollie's pronouns are they and them*, Dad had said that morning before I'd left the house. I'd heard of that; an eighth-grader back home used they/them pronouns. *Look out for them*, he'd encouraged. *They could be a friend.* I'd nodded while internally rolling my eyes at the idea that having a random connection to one out of hundreds of people at a new school could make anything about this move less terrible.

"They weren't in any of my morning classes," I replied.

I could tell by Dad's wrinkled brow that he felt sorry. About everything. And I knew I should tell him that it was okay. That I'd settle in and the semester would be fine. But I couldn't. Or I wouldn't. And I wasn't sure which made me feel worse.

The doorbell rang, saving me from the need to say more. "Let's go, Dad," I said. "Pizza's here."

Outside, we sat on the peeling front porch steps, the pizza

box between us. North Carolina was a different kind of August-hot than Saint Louis, and humidity draped invisibly from the overhang, southern-style. My thighs stuck to the steps. Two blocks from not-home, I envisioned the dim, after-school hallways at South Campus Lab School and laid my half-eaten pizza slice onto a napkin. More than anything else, I'd been dreading my first lunch period as the "new girl" ever since April, when Mom and Dad had broken the news.

"Your dad can't pass up this visiting professorship," Mom had said plainly when they'd sat me down on our living room couch.

"And you can't stay here; Mom's work is too unpredictable right now," he had chimed in.

"Mom, you're *self-employed*," I'd reminded her. "Couldn't you just move your art studio to North Carolina for four months?"

Silence.

"That's easier said than done," she'd finally replied. "Besides, it's just for the semester."

108 DAYS LEFT

I shivered in my tank top as I approached the lunchroom. The first full day of school the day before had been depressing, to say the least. I'd felt totally distracted the entire day. I knew that I couldn't hide out at the back table again, feeling awkward and sorry for myself, thinking about Emily, Ava, and Beth back home; the lunch table we always sat at; how easy it had been, every day, to walk into the cafeteria and know that the third table to the left of the hot lunch window was *our* table.

I froze in the doorway of the lunchroom, not used to putting myself out there. Emily and I had become best friends in kindergarten. Ava and Beth had joined our group in fifth grade. It had literally been two years since I'd gone through the motions of making a new friend. This exact situation was what I'd been dreading for five months.

I scanned the tables anxiously. Just as I was about to give

up and head to the back table again, I heard my name. "Essie!" A girl named Savannah from some of my classes was waving me over to her table.

"Oh my God, thanks," I said, approaching her. "You just saved me from eating alone. Being new sucks," I admitted.

"Believe me, I know," she said, patting the open seat next to her. "That was me last year." I smiled to myself at her southern accent. It was different. *Cool.*

I didn't even have a chance to ask where she'd moved from. She began introducing me to the seventh graders who flocked to our table with lunch trays and canvas bags as the cafeteria filled. The vibe wasn't all that different from what I was accustomed to. The students were diverse, just like back home. Savannah was Black. A girl named Luciana, who seemed to be one of her good friends, appeared Latina. "Don't worry if you can't remember everyone's name," Savannah reassured me.

Diagonally from me, a boy took a seat, confident at a table of girls. He was white like me, with sandy brown hair and blue, blue eyes. My eyes caught his as I turned to my sandwich, and I felt a weird, electric jolt. When I looked back up, he was smiling at me. "And that's Ollie," Luciana said, smiling across the table.

Ollie.

106 DAYS LEFT

It turned out that I had art, and then science, with Ollie after lunch. How had I not noticed them the day before? I couldn't stop thinking about them throughout dinner with Dad at an Indian place near campus that, according to Marianne, had the best curry in the world. (Mom hates curry.) I'd never felt that *jolt* before. And it had never crossed my mind that I might feel it for someone whose pronouns weren't he/him.

Earlier that day, I'd watched them from across the cluttered art room. They'd gotten up from their paint-spattered table to rummage through supplies, continually running their hand through their hair (long, flopping into their eyes on top, short underneath). Tiny gold hoops hung from their perfect ear-lobes; their gray hoodie draped loosely over camo shorts.

Maybe they'd sensed me looking, because they'd glanced

over their shoulder and grinned. I'd smiled at them, and then at my half-sketched still life of an apple.

Dad and I returned from dinner. He deposited our leftovers in the fridge, and I flopped on the couch to text Emily for the first time since that Tuesday, when I'd told her how depressing it had been to sit alone in the cafeteria.

Essie **Emily**

Waasup Em!

> Hiiiiiiii stranger!

Have u forgotten me

> Have YOU forgotten ME

Impossible. So things r looking up i've met some nice ppl especially someone named ollie

> OMGGGGGGGG
> that was fast.

> Last time u texted u told me u were hopping the train back home. Ollie! Is he cute

Haha yes! Things r better

> Phew! Keep me posted!!!

Kk

I read back over the text exchange not knowing why I didn't tell Emily what Ollie's pronouns were. She'd definitely be cool with them. Not telling her wasn't about Ollie; it was about me. My brain felt like a tangle of wires. I tried to ignore the fact that they lit up whenever I envisioned Ollie's face.

102 DAYS LEFT

Standing on my unmade bed, I drew the fourth line of my second tally. I'd made it through Week One *and* Labor Day weekend.

Okay. So things weren't as terrible as they could have been. The girls at school, Savannah and Luciana especially, were nice. I liked the electricity that I felt around Ollie. It wasn't the same as being with friends I'd had since elementary school, but it was definitely manageable.

Morning sun splashed the tiny kitchen. Dad would have freaked to see me pour coffee into one of our Saint Louis Cardinals mugs, but he was in the bathroom. (Back home, Mom and I had kept my coffee habit *our little secret*.) I added milk and sugar and took a sip. The kitchen opened into a tiny furnished living room where everything was beige. Across from our two minuscule bedrooms, the toilet flushed.

A bird chirped outside the open window, and I wondered if Ollie had left for school yet. I took my coffee onto the front porch.

Inside, Dad bustled around the kitchen until it was time for us to leave. I stowed my empty mug under the porch swing. At the corner, he ruffled my hair and turned left. I turned right, pulled out my fig-colored lip gloss, and ran it smoothly over my lips.

At school, Savannah, Luciana, and some other girls sat on the stone steps that rose toward the arched wooden doors. I hoped nobody would ask about my weekend (which had involved watching subtitled films with Dad, eating Thai food with Dad, and browsing Target with Dad).

I joined the girls on the steps. Savannah's beaded braids swung as she turned to me. "Hey, Essie! How was your weekend?"

"It was boring," I admitted. "Hey, where did *you* move here from?" I asked, trying to divert attention from my pathetic social life.

"Atlanta. My mom got a new job at the university. So . . ."

"My dad, too. Well, he's doing a visiting professorship. I spent the weekend hanging out with him," I confessed.

"It's only the two of you?"

I nodded. "Since we're just here for the semester, my mom stayed back in Saint Louis. She couldn't come because of work, and I couldn't stay with her because she travels too much."

"What does she do?"

"She's an artist. She does installation pieces." Savannah looked confused, which was something I was used to when it came to explaining Mom's job. "Her latest piece is at this model recycling plant in Seattle. She made a *T. rex* skeleton for their front entryway out of, like, garbage."

Savannah raised her eyebrows.

"Yeah, old, cut-up yogurt containers and stuff."

"Oh. So when she's not traveling, does she work in a studio or something?"

I nodded. "It's at home. In our basement," I said, wondering if Savannah was thinking the same thing I was: If Mom really wanted to come with us, she could have made it happen.

Savannah opened her mouth to say something, then closed it. I looked to my shoes, then to where Ollie was making their way toward us. They flipped their hair out of their eyes and smiled at us.

Zap.

101 DAYS LEFT

Gym class at Lab could have been gym class back home. The track was spongy after morning rains, and the low gray sky trapped the humid air. I'd never minded running.

Luciana, Savannah, and I pounded out synchronized rhythms with damp shoes as, across the field, teachers supervised the girls doing high jump and discus. Boys were stuck with health class this week.

"Did some people get added to our P.E. section?" Savannah panted, pointing to the building door where a few people in green Lab gym shirts had appeared.

"Yeah, a math class got switched, and it messed up a few schedules. Ollie was telling me in homeroom," Luciana said.

After gym, back in the locker room, I bent over the water fountain for a long time, then went to my locker to change. Savannah and Luciana sat, backs to me, in sports bras and gym shorts, changing their shoes. In front of them, wearing a baggy green shirt, green shorts, and soccer socks, was Ollie. We smiled at each other as their eyes, black-rimmed blue, met mine.

That afternoon, I completed the second tally on my wall and checked my phone. Emily had texted: *How's Ollie?!*

I wandered into the kitchen. Leaves rustled in the warm air outside the open window. I turned on the ceiling fan. How's Ollie? I didn't know how to respond. I wanted Emily to know everything about my crush. I just didn't want to have to tell her this new thing about myself. I wished I could telepathically transmit the message to her: *I like someone with they/them pronouns! It's no big deal even though how I feel around Ollie seems like a Big Deal.*

I shoved my phone under a pile of junk mail on the kitchen counter, imagining Ollie's face again and feeling the familiar twinkle of electricity.

Outside, afternoon shadows flickered on the front steps. I watched them as I sat on the creaking porch swing, wondering what Mom was doing. She hadn't called for a couple of days. Classic Mom. I knew she was busy planning a new piece for a gallery in New York, but most likely, she hadn't called because she was trying to "give me my independence," something she'd gotten big on once I'd started middle school the year before.

And finally, I allowed myself to think of Ollie, because I kind of couldn't help it. I'd had crushes before. Lots. But this one felt, well, *different*.

99 DAYS LEFT

It was weird that I didn't *really* talk to Ollie until my second week at Lab.

In the locker room, I ignored the smiles that Savannah and Luciana exchanged when Ollie said hi to me.

"Hey," I replied, way too aware of the blood pumping through my veins.

They turned their back to change, pulled their green T-shirt over their sports bra, and sat on the bench next to me to tie their shoelaces, their longer, top layer of hair falling across their face. They seemed kind of shy, which was cute. I was curious about their gender, and I wondered if that made me nosy.

Once we were dressed, Ollie and I trailed Savannah and Luciana into the gym, where we were directed to partner up. Luciana turned quickly to Savannah. Ollie and I made eye contact and smiled.

* * *

That night, after a dinner of leftover takeout, Dad and I walked toward campus to a place called Jak's. According to Marianne, it had the best ice cream in town. My stomach flip-flopped when I saw Ollie sitting on a bench with a woman I assumed was their mom, licking a cone.

"Hey, Ollie," I said, grinning.

"What are you doing here?" they asked.

"You know, ice cream."

They laughed.

"Hi there!" Dad said to Ollie's mom. He turned to me. "You didn't tell me you and Ollie had met!" I shrugged.

"Hey, fellow humans!" Ollie's mom chimed in. "I see you took my advice to try Jak's!"

Dad put his arm around my shoulder. "Marianne, this is Esther—"

"Essie," I interrupted.

"Nice to meet you, Essie," Marianne said. "Walter, meet my kiddo, Ollie."

"Ollie," Dad said, extending his hand.

Ollie shook it.

We got our ice cream and Dad joined Marianne on the bench, where they jumped right into an intense discussion about whether to cancel the course on urban systems due to low enrollment (snore).

"You have to see something," Ollie told me, and they pulled me across the street, in the direction of the campus. At the end of the block, outside a restaurant called Satter's Platters and next to a water bowl, stood two real, live spotted pigs. Their leashes were looped through a nearby bike rack.

"Are you serious?" I asked.

Ollie laughed. "Totally serious."

The pigs snorted.

A waiter in a blue apron walked out of the restaurant just as Ollie squatted and extended their hand toward the pigs, who proceeded to lick their fingers as the waiter looked on.

"They obviously don't mind pig slobber," I said to the waiter, making conversation.

"A little slobber could never interfere with Ollie, Panda, and Penelope's relationship," he responded, grinning at us, as I reluctantly reached my hand toward the pigs's snouts to pet them.

Eyes shining, Ollie wiggled their eyebrows at me. "Small town."

"I'm glad you're cool with them," Ollie had said after Panda and Penelope had finished licking our fingers. "Some people aren't."

"Honestly, I can't understand bigots like that," I'd told them, relieved that they'd brought up their pronouns. I'd wanted an opportunity to tell them I was cool with their gender, even though they probably already knew.

Ollie had looked at me kind of strangely. "I get it," they'd said. "I don't love *all* farm animals. I mean, chickens and roosters are just weird. The wattles hanging from their necks? So gross."

Suddenly, I'd had no idea what we were talking about. "What?" I'd asked.

"What?" they'd repeated, as we'd stopped walking. The sun had lowered behind us, golden rays glowing through wilted leaves.

"I . . . I thought you meant you were glad I'm cool with your pronouns," I'd stammered, my face flushing with embarrassment, realizing that Ollie wouldn't be here with me otherwise. "But you meant—"

"The pigs," Ollie had said, finishing my thought, trying to hide their smile. "I meant I'm glad you're cool with the pigs. 'Cause, you know . . . some people aren't." I could tell they wanted to laugh, but not in a mean way.

"I'm such an idiot," I'd said, smiling a little, rubbing my fingertips (sticky with pig slobber) as I'd looked at them. Their smooth skin, leftover summer tan, and eyes—glinting blue. "I'm sorry."

Did words exist for my feelings? I didn't know.

After school, Ollie was waiting at my locker.

"Want a job?" they asked, grinning.

"Hello to you, too."

"Please?" they fake begged, clasping their hands together. "We have approximately one billion posters to hang up." They dropped their backpack onto the ground and dug out a stack of papers.

"What are they for?" I asked, looking through the pages of bright, bubble-lettered cardstock.

"GLOW Club," Ollie said. "Gender and Love Open-minded Warriors. We're going to erase all the hate in the world."

"I hate hate," I told them. "So it's like a GSA?" We had a Genders and Sexualities Alliance back home. I'd never paid much attention to it.

"Yeah, just with a much better name. So you'll help?"

"Sure!"

I threw my backpack into my locker, and Ollie, Savannah, Luciana, and I hung posters around school while some of the other members of the club went off to brainstorm fundraising ideas.

"We have to publicize *and* recruit more members," Ollie said when we all met on the stone steps at four. "We only have *seven* participants." Before I could say a word, they turned to me, grinning. "I know you're just here till December. But yes, including you."

Emily

Helloooooo stranger it's your long-lost friend Emily Suzuki.

Remember me?

> Don't hate me. Plz.

Impossible

> I have a confession

You have a new best friend?

> Never

Phew

I'm waiting

OMG OLLIE!

> Omg Ollie

You're in love!

I learned something that I didn't tell u. So . . .
Ollie isn't a boy

I'm so confused

Ollie's pronouns are they/them

Oh.
Wait what?

Like Morgan, in 8th grade

OH!

What do you think?

What do you mean?

Does it make me weird?

Who cares!
Maybe he's nonbinary
*Their
*They're

Hang on . . . looking up nonbinary

Do there parents support them
OMG *their

Lol I think so? I've only met their mom. She works with my dad

Sociologist? I'm sure she's a hippie

Probably. Ran into them at ice cream and she was wearing Birkenstocks so I'm sure she's supportive

OMG you're gonna have ur 1st kiss in NC!

OMG I ♥ you

And I won't be there to talk to you about it. ☹

We can FaceTime?

Not the same. This is no fun with you gone.

Xoxo

Xoxo xoxo

92 DAYS LEFT

Ollie had no problem recruiting seven additional people, so, in total, fourteen of us attended the first GLOW lunch meeting on Friday. Ms. Rose, the faculty sponsor, plopped a bag of colorful, rainbow-shaped erasers onto the table among our lunch bags and trays.

"Yay, they came!" Ollie said, jumping up and riffling through the bag. "Ms. Rose and I ordered them forever ago," they explained, taking a few and passing the bag to a sixth grader with a pink streak in his hair.

"They started this club," an eighth grader told me, referring to Ollie. "At the beginning of last year."

Ollie shrugged at us. "It's no big deal," they said.

I thought it was. It was awesome.

"We can pass them out starting Monday," Ollie told everyone, referring to the rainbow erasers. "As publicity, and to pique *more* interest," they said. "We need as many new members as we can get."

I wondered how many new members Ollie was hoping for. Fourteen people seemed pretty good for a school club. Back home, the GSA was way smaller.

That night, after Dad's four o'clock class, I met him at the Indian restaurant. Again.

"We should eat as much Indian as possible before going home," he said once we'd ordered.

"Do you even *want* to go home?" I asked impulsively. As soon as the question settled over us, I knew I wouldn't get the type of answer I was hoping for.

"This is a fun adventure," he replied evasively. "Do *you* want to go home?"

"Obviously," I answered quickly, but then thought of Ollie. "Well, when the time comes."

Dad smiled, unwrapping two Lactaid pills.

"But do you . . . ?" I didn't know how to finish. *Do you miss Mom?* I didn't need to ask him to know the answer was *no*. Mom and Dad *coexisted*; they definitely didn't seem in love with each other. Not, for example, like Emily's parents, who were constantly kissing and hugging each other, did. As far as I knew, he and Mom had barely even talked since we'd moved. So I settled on "Do you like this job better than your job back home?"

"It's different," he replied. "Apples and oranges."

Talking to Dad was like avoiding words, avoiding labels for what he wanted, what he felt. It always had been, unless he was discussing sociology. So I asked him about his classes, and he talked and talked about the statistical significance of a study on rural education until our food arrived.

91 DAYS LEFT

I stood in front of the bathroom mirror brushing my hair. Ollie was coming over; the day before, we'd made plans to draw even *more* GLOW posters.

"You mean one billion isn't enough?" I'd joked as we'd stood on the steps together after school, the afternoon sun beating onto the sides of our heads. We'd waved to Luciana and Savannah as they had headed off to an informational meeting about the volleyball team.

"Definitely not," they'd replied seriously. "We should hang some in the Lower School, too. Maybe we can get some fifth graders involved."

Now we sat together on the front porch among Crayola markers and strewn poster board. They caught me watching as they drew a rainbow. "You're a good artist," they said, snapping the cap onto the purple marker.

"Thanks." I eyed their uneven lettering. "Um, you too?"

Ollie laughed. "Shut up," they joked, rubbing the smear of ink on the side of their hand.

The front door opened and Dad came out with my phone. "Hey, guys," he said, holding the phone out to me. "It's Mom."

Mom. I hadn't told Ollie much about her. Just that she was planning a giant installation of scrap metal falling through a hole in the drywall of a New York gallery's ceiling. Like *that* was normal. I took the phone. "Hey, Mom."

Ollie looked on curiously as Dad returned to the air-conditioning inside.

"Hey, Es! Just checking in. It's been a few days."

Four days, to be exact. So maybe I'd been testing her, just to see how long she'd wait before calling. How independent did she really think I should be? "Yeah, hi," I said, opening a yellow marker and drawing an *I'm annoyed* emoji face with a straight mouth on the back of my hand. I held it up for Ollie to see. They laughed.

"How's life? I haven't heard from you, so you must be having fun."

"I am, actually," I told her as Ollie drew a red face with a zigzag smile on the back of their hand for me. I giggled. Even though I'd been waiting for Mom to call for four days, I didn't feel like talking to her. "I'm actually kind of working on something for school with a friend. Can I call you later?"

"Sure, great. Call whenever. I don't want to interfere."

I rolled my eyes, said goodbye, and looked from Ollie's hand to their perfect face. "My mom . . . ," I started.

"Yeah?" I felt like I could tell them anything in the world.

"She's just . . . aloof," I finally finished.

They looked guilty. "I know," they admitted. "My mom kind of told me. Are you mad?"

Mad? I wasn't mad. I was surprised—that Dad had talked to Marianne about Mom at all.

Several GLOW posters later, I walked Ollie to the corner, the sudden wind blowing in humid gusts against our backs. "My mom wasn't always so distant," I told them. "She used to be really involved."

"What changed?" they asked, holding tightly to the poster boards as they flapped in the wind.

"I went to middle school."

"And?"

I laughed, even though it was more weird than funny. "I don't know. I think she wanted to give me my freedom. Her parents were really controlling when she was a teenager. She used to tell me stories about sneaking out her window to see friends because she was supposed to stay home and study all the time. Maybe she's trying to do the opposite with me?"

"Wait, her parents wouldn't let her leave the house? That sucks," Ollie confirmed.

"Right? But it's also kind of dumb to do the polar opposite."

"That's true," Ollie agreed, waiting for me to go on. But I didn't feel like talking anymore about the way that Mom was, for the past year, suddenly *uninvolved* in my life.

"I was wondering," I said, "fourteen members is pretty good for GLOW, isn't it? I mean, back home there were only five or six people in our GSA. When do we stop trying to get more members and move on to, you know, other stuff?"

Ollie slowed and their face hardened as if, suddenly, they were . . . something. Mad? Disappointed?

"Are you okay?" I asked.

"Yeah, I'm good," they finally said. "You're right. Fourteen *is* a great number. It's just . . ." The wind gusted, fluttering the poster boards again. "I guess it's hard to explain."

I watched them, waiting for more. Wanting more. But they stayed quiet.

Explain it anyway, I wanted to say. But I didn't know how. "Okay," I said. "So I guess I'll see you Monday?"

They nodded, waved, and were gone.

90 DAYS LEFT

Essie

Emily

Help Em

What's up

I think I ruined something

Okay

Stop being so calm.
HELP!

Fine, what did you ruin?

Things with Ollie feel
weird

DID YOU KISS THEM?

OMG shut up. No

Bummer

I think they're mad at me

No! What happened?

Yesterday I said
something . . .

Something dumb?

Apparently. I asked about
the GSA

GLOW, the club they're
president of

Oh yeah I told you

Duh

I asked why we needed
more members. There are
14. Seems like a lot right?

Makes sense

Then they seemed mad

Weird. Ask them? Don't
be a wimp remember
before u left u were
saying u wanted to like
put ur self out there
more

I did?

Dummy

Ok

Keep me posted

Essie

Ollie

Hey Ollie

Waasup

Nothing. You?

Nothing.

Can I ask u something?

Yes

R u mad at me?

Not mad . . . That would
be the wrong word

Definitely not mad.
Disappointed?

☹ What did I do? I'm sorry

It's complicated. Too
hard to explain over text.

FaceTime?

Come over tomorrow
after school?

Definitely

89 DAYS LEFT

"Rabbits are stupid substitutes for dogs," Ollie said as we sat, looking at each other through their bunny's cage on the living room floor. Then, by way of introduction, "Essie, meet my furry sister Froggy. Froggy, meet Essie."

"*Froggy?*" I asked, laughing, as the bunny wiggled her nose at me.

"Rabbits hop, frogs hop . . . Hey, I was in fourth grade when I named her. Don't judge me."

"She's cute," I told Ollie, sticking my finger through the bars of the cage to rub Froggy's ear.

"I agree. She's no dog, but she's cute." Ollie opened the cage and scooped Froggy out as I looked over the bunny's ears to them—their backward black baseball cap, gold hoops. Their eyes.

They sighed. "So we've never actually talked about it—the gender stuff. You know. Who I am. What it's like."

I didn't know what to say. Was that a good thing, that we hadn't talked about it? Or did that mean Ollie was mad that I'd never brought it up?

"It's just that I sort of have to be an advocate sometimes. Like, raise awareness and educate people, which can be exhausting and annoying. But at the same time, I kind of love it. It's weird."

"I get that."

"And I have to bring people together, so nobody feels *alone*," they went on, handing Froggy over to me. Her fuzzy nose twitched as she settled into my lap. "I mean, people need to know that lots of people like me exist," Ollie continued emphatically. "I'm not *that* unique."

"Okay." It made sense. "You just always seem so comfortable with yourself. I didn't think the gender thing was an issue for you."

Smiling, Ollie took off their cap. "It's not."

Froggy jumped off my lap and Ollie handed me a strand of dusty alfalfa to feed her.

"But you seemed annoyed when I asked about GLOW membership. I'm confused," I admitted.

"Can we be confused together?"

"Forever."

"Or," Ollie said, blushing, "at least until you ditch me in December."

* * *

After Marianne fed us cookies and lemonade, Ollie walked
me home so they could borrow my math notes.

"Sorry about the mess," I said, leading them past the coffee table, piled high with Dad's grading, and into my bedroom for my notebook.

"Whoa," Ollie said, stopping in the doorway, staring at the
twenty-two tally marks on my wall.

"It's a nice prison," they went on, looking at my overflow-
ing closet and unmade bed.

I laughed.

"The warden must trust you—no bars on the windows,"
they continued.

"My dad is a complete space cadet. I could get away
with anything," I said, surprising myself because there
had never been anything I'd been eager to *get away with*
before.

"Really?" They looked excited. "Have you ever taken advantage of that?"

"Nah. I'm boring."

"Yeah, me, too." There was a moment of silence. Ollie
moved a pile of folded-but-not-put-away clothes and
sat on my desk as I lay back against my wrinkled pillows. "So you really want to get out of here, huh?" they
asked.

I didn't. Not anymore. Maybe making the tally marks had just become a habit. But I felt like Ollie was kind of asking me if I liked them, and I didn't want to tell them the truth until I knew they liked me, too. So, in classic Essie fashion, I just shrugged.

Ollie

Essie

Hi!

Hey!

Is the warden on duty?

If sleeping on the couch under a stack of essays with a red pen dangling from his hand = on duty then yes

Do u think u could escape?

Really?!

Have u seen the moon?

No!

Look out ur window.

Kk

Omg that is amazing it's orange!

Meet me at the corner?

For real?! One sec I better wake the warden and ask

U mean u don't have to sneak out like ur mom did?

Haha unlikely
See you in 5!

See ya!

"You got out of prison!" Ollie confirmed happily when I met them at the corner.

"Not before drawing another line on the wall," I joked.

"Funny." They didn't look like they thought it was funny, though, and that made me selfishly happy. Maybe I had zapped them, too. "Turn around."

Over the rooftops, in the crook of a tree branch, hung an orange, glowing half-moon. "Whoa, that's incredible," I told Ollie, pulling up my hood. The late September nighttime air was finally cool.

They grinned proudly.

"We need lawn chairs or something so we can sit and look at it!" I told them. "No, a hammock!"

"We *so* need a hammock."

87 DAYS LEFT

I'd known Ollie for three weeks, but I didn't *know them* know them. I mean, I knew *certain* things:

Their pronouns were *they* and *them*. Maybe they were non-binary. I'd read up on stuff online.

They were an advocate because they had to be and, also, because they wanted to be.

They'd told me other important things: Luciana had been their best friend forever. They got along with their parents. Like, really well. They wanted, no, *needed*, a dog.

So yes, I knew some things about them. But I wanted to *know* them.

"I have a question," I said as we sat on the porch swing after school, watching the September drizzle.

"Crap."

"Why 'crap'?"

"You want to talk about my gender, right?"

"No!" I said quickly.

Ollie looked at me sideways.

"Yes."

"I knew it. Everyone wants the lowdown eventually."

"Is that annoying?" I asked.

"Totally. But not with you," they added immediately, not looking at me. "*You* can ask me anything."

Zap.

I thought back to what I'd read online. "So you were assigned female at birth?" Even though Ollie had said I could ask them anything, I felt nervous as the words left my mouth; I'd never had a conversation like this before.

At first, Ollie didn't respond, and I felt my face flush. But then they turned to me. Smiled. "Have you been on the internet?" they asked.

"Maybe?"

"Yeah," they answered. "For a long time, I was fine being called a tomboy."

"And you're sure you're not a boy? A trans boy, I mean?"

"Do you wish I were a boy?"

"I don't," I answered quickly. And I meant it. Now that I *knew* Ollie, I couldn't imagine them as anything other than who they were.

"I'm not a boy; I'm a girl who's a boy."

I nodded, because knowing Ollie, that made sense to me. "Are you gender queer?"

"I'm *definitely* gender *weird*." They made eye contact with me. Wiggled their eyebrows. Smiled.

"Are you nonbinary, then?"

"Yeah." They swung their leg. Impatient.

"Are you okay?"

"Definitely. Can you hurry up, though?"

"Hurry up and what?"

"And get used to it, so I can just be Ollie?"

I thought of advocate-Ollie. "Do you *want* to just be Ollie?"

They laughed. "Sometimes." Then they added, "When I'm with you, I do."

86 DAYS LEFT

Ollie, Savannah, Luciana, and I walked out the front doors of school into the muggy three-o'clock air. In unison, we dropped our backpacks to peel off our sweatshirts. The shift from full-blast AC to sunny September afternoons in North Carolina was brutal.

"You babysitting for your brothers, Lucy?" Ollie asked, shoving their sweatshirt into their backpack. They smelled like clean laundry.

"No. Remember, *someone* talked me into joining volleyball?" Luciana joked, narrowing her eyes at Savannah. "We have practice. The *only* upside is less babysitting for Carlos and Diego."

Savannah grinned. "Hey, you're getting better," she said. "Remember yesterday, when you didn't squat down and cover your head when the ball came your way?"

We all laughed.

"Are you walking home?" Ollie asked, nudging me.

"Yup," I said, digging my phone out of my backpack. We waved to Luciana and Savannah as they headed off toward the athletics building. Ollie and I made our way to the sidewalk, and I thought (again) about our conversation the day before:

They didn't always want to be just-Ollie, but with me, they did.

What did that mean? I mean, I *thought* I knew what it meant, but I wanted to know for sure; I wanted them to put more words with it. I wanted *labels* for the feelings—theirs *and* mine.

"Essie?" Ollie waved their hand in front of my face as if it wasn't the first time they'd said my name. "Were you thinking about me?" they asked jokingly, the afternoon sun making their blue eyes bluer.

"Obviously," I replied (not) jokingly.

I turned my phone on. There were a few texts from Ava and Beth, who I'd totally neglected since arriving in North Carolina. And I'd just missed a call from Mom. I sighed and held it up so Ollie could see that I had a voicemail from her.

"A message from the free-range mother!" They grinned.

"Seriously," I replied, playing the voicemail.

Hey, Es, it's Mom. Just calling to say hi. Call back whenever you want. Love you!

It was weird that, beyond the few, surface things I'd relayed to her, Mom didn't know *anything* about my life in North Carolina. Unless she'd talked to Dad recently, which I seriously doubted. In fact, the other day I *might* have scrolled through his phone, confirming that they basically never texted or called each other.

It was an accurate label that Ollie had used for Mom: a *free-range mother*.

I could label Dad easily. He was *spacey. Sort of out-of-touch*. But definitely *nice*.

What about their marriage? What was the label for that? *Over?*

"Do you want to call her back?" Ollie asked, adjusting their backpack.

I didn't. "Nah, I'll call her later."

"Okay."

We walked awhile in silence.

"Hey, so, according to the interweb, the moon should be completely awesome again tonight," Ollie said kind of awkwardly, looping their thumbs through their backpack straps, sneaking a glance at me.

I smiled, thinking of a hammock hanging from a September

tree and how I kind of definitely wanted to kiss Ollie. And then thinking of whether it should matter to me that I wanted to kiss someone who was nonbinary. I mean, if Ollie and I kissed, them being nonbinary wouldn't *matter* matter. But it *would* matter, because it was who they were. And, more important, because it would mean something about who I was.

"Will the warden let you out tonight?" they asked.

"Only after I clean the bathroom floor with a toothbrush."

"Scrub quickly and meet me at eight?"

"Deal."

Essie

Em! Plz tell me you're there

I'm here!

Thank god.

omg did you kiss Ollie?!

No but I think I almost kissed Ollie

Last nite

AAAHHHHHHHH!!!!!

Was that happy or angry?

Both?

I know.

Tell me everything

WAITING

ESSIE

Sorry my dad was talking logistics of who is showering first and that we have to go to the grocery store

TALK

We met at the corner

AND?

Geez. Because there was a cool moon again. Did I tell u they're into the moon? Anyway, they said to follow them. Oh, last time we'd been saying it would be awesome to have a hammock to look at the moon from.

This is so adorable!

Shut up. So they took me to their neighbor's yard. We kind of snuck in thru the bushes because they have a hammock.

And we hung out in it together.

It was nice.

But no kiss?

No.

Crap

Crap. What's up with you?

Gotta facetime Ava & Beth.

Group project.

Txt more later?

Definitely. Will u tell them hi and sorry I'm a horrible person for neglecting them and I'll facetime them soon?

Done

xo

84 DAYS LEFT

It was eleven fifteen on Saturday night. I couldn't sleep. The streetlight outside my bedroom window cast a wavering glow onto my wall. Shadows of branches danced like weird, willowy people over my head. I looked at the completed tally sets on my wall. They didn't mean what they used to. My time in North Carolina was one-fourth over.

I thought of how, back at Jak's, Marianne had addressed me, Ollie, and Dad as "fellow humans." If we were all just *people* and gender didn't exist for me or Ollie, would we have kissed in the hammock? The view of the moon through the tree branches had been perfect. Our shoulders had pressed together as we'd lain side by side. The backs of our hands had been touching. The zaps had become a force field surrounding us.

What *were* the zaps, anyway? I wondered. They felt like electric beginnings or effervescing doors, rimmed in rows and rows of twinkling fairy lights and constructed of glowing specks of warm, North Carolina air. In my mind, when I'd reach for the doorknob, the lights would rain down into a carpet of red and gold leaves and radiant sunlight. The door would disappear.

And Ollie would be standing there.

And I'd ask them: Can you feel it, too?

I got my phone. Ollie had texted at 10:51 P.M.: *You up?*

Essie　　　　　　　　　　　　　**Ollie**

Hey! You still there?

> Yup

I can't sleep

> I know

Why is gender a thing?

> What do you mean?

Why does it matter?

> I half love/half hate that question

I kinda get what u mean

> Hang out tomorrow night?

It's a date

83 DAYS LEFT

The sun was lowering behind the swings at the park. Ollie and I had walked to Jak's for ice cream. Now, as we pumped our legs in unison, I tried to visualize Ollie playing on the jungle gym in front of us when they were a little kid. How did they look as a five-year-old? A ten-year-old? Even though Ollie had told me they used to be okay with a "tomboy" label, I realized how much I didn't know about them. Did they ever have long hair? Wear "girls' clothes"? Would they be okay with me wondering these things? Or should I just think about who they are now?

"Essie?" Ollie interrupted my thoughts, and I turned to them quickly. The sun created a halo around their hair. Every strand was illuminated. "Want to . . ." *Do something?* *About the zaps?* ". . . come to the spinny-spin with me?"

"What's a spinny-spin?" I asked, laughing, jumping off my still-swinging swing.

"That thing." They pointed to the royal-blue, rotating playground structure that had probably made a bunch of kids puke over the years. "Spin with me?" They jumped off their swing. Landed by my side. Held out their hand.

I took it.

On the spinny-spin, I lay on my back, my head in the center of the rusted, sandy circle. Ollie ran it around, jumped on, and rested their head beside mine. They looked at me.

Above us, the darkening sky whirled in circles. I knew the kiss was coming, but instead of feeling excited, I started to feel . . . panicky. Because the truth is, you can never know *for sure* how someone feels about you. I mean, it definitely *seemed* like Ollie liked me, but how could I know for real? Mom and Dad had probably really liked each other once, too. And Mom and I had been so close until she'd basically decided that I was "all grown up."

I searched Ollie's face in the dying light for the blue of their eyes as thick air seemed to weave a cocoon through the spinny-spin's rails. Inside the cocoon, it seemed safer, a place where I wouldn't have to worry about whether anyone's feelings were for real. So I pulled myself in, just as Ollie kissed me.

82 DAYS LEFT

My alarm chimed, and I felt frantically beneath my covers for my phone. I scanned my texts. Again. Still nothing.

The stretch of tallies over my bed had seemed to be rushing toward December just the day before. Now my eyes drifted to the white space to the right of the marks; I still had three months left. I opened my Sharpie and made my twenty-ninth line. For the first time in weeks, I wanted to go home.

It was clear that, on Ollie's end, something was wrong; the kiss had obviously been weird for them, too. I'd only been able to focus on the warm, humid cocoon. There had been no electric charge on that frayed wire inside of me, the way there'd been when I'd first seen Ollie. And every second of every day after that. There'd been no zaps. No force field.

And besides, now that we'd kissed, I couldn't stop wondering: If Ollie was nonbinary and I liked them, what did that make me? Partly it made me annoyed to have to think about it. I was just me, just-Essie. But also, what was my label?

It was as if, with all the emotions I had, there was no room left in my brain for words. Half of me was desperate to see Ollie at school, and the other half dreaded it. Savannah and Luciana would definitely know that *something* had happened. When I saw Ollie, everything would feel strange and wrong.

In the end, it didn't matter, because they didn't show up.

After school, I texted Emily.

Hey Em we kissed. Things r weird. I rly like them. Also what does this make me. Like what is my label?

She was probably at soccer; she didn't respond.

81 DAYS LEFT

At school the next day, I watched for Ollie as I walked through the halls. Did I want to see them? Avoid them? I didn't know. I was aware of my every move. Each second of the morning, I stood in Ollie's shoes and looked at myself. Was the way I walked stupid? How about the way I picked up my backpack?

I finally saw them in the hallway between third and fourth periods. They looked away quickly as we approached each other, but then smiled at me. Forced? Fake?

"Hey," they said, stopping amid students pushing their way to classes.

"Hey."

Then, like nothing had happened, they half said, half asked, "See you at lunch?" and walked away.

I stood, frozen, in the current of people, watching them go.

So this was how it was going to be; we were going to pretend nothing had happened. Pretend that we hadn't kissed. And I was going to pretend that whatever my label was didn't matter? (Did it matter?)

GLOW was meeting at lunch, and as we sat around the table, I struggled to focus. Ollie was talking about an idea they had come up with: a GLOW event sponsored by the university's Sociology Department, on campus, the week after Thanksgiving. "A Thanksgiving Thankful for Pride event!"

"That's such a great idea," Luciana told Ollie. They smiled at each other.

I agreed. And I loved watching advocate-Ollie talk about it.

But I also missed just-Ollie. Just-Ollie from the hammock, three days before we'd kissed, moonlit, hand against my hand, pointing to the stars overhead.

Essie

Emily

Em! Wassup!

Don't hate me. I'm an awful friend

3 tests this week. Sry didn't text back

I haven't had a single test yet!

I wanna transfer to ur school

Please!!!!!

Everyone's asking about you! Have you talked to anyone else?!

Not really. I've been a horrible friend to Beth

and Ava and had to turn
off notifications on the
7th grade girls chat. It's
outta control

Totally out of control!

So Beth and Ava wanna
know what's up!

Can I tell them?

About Ollie?

Yeah and about you

What about me?

What you texted
last time. Sorry I
didn't respond.
Tests . . .

Oh. No. I'll tell
them

OK, you should text
them! They keep asking
me how you are

I'm on it

Cool! So what's going on?

Things are still weird
with Ollie

Post-kiss weird?

Perfect! see u in an hour!

??

Omg sry texting Ava too!

ha

OK gotta run xoxo

xo

78 DAYS LEFT

After school, I texted Dad that I couldn't do "Indian Food Friday" with him. After lunch, Ollie had invited me over to plan for the Thankful for Pride event. They'd gotten a haircut. I'd wanted to touch the extra-spiky soft hairs beneath the long strands that were falling over their eyes.

Waiting on the front steps, I tucked my phone into my backpack as Luciana and Savannah approached me. "Hey!" they said, both zipping up against the cold-for-North-Carolina breeze.

"You're coming to Ollie's, too, right?" Savannah asked.

The world tilted, then righted itself. "Oh, right." I guess it was stupid of me to have thought it was going to be just the two of us.

I wondered, again, what Luciana and Savannah knew about me and Ollie. I was sure that, at the very least, Ollie had told Luciana everything. But, if Luciana knew things were awkward, she wasn't letting on.

Above us, the arched doors opened and Ollie came down the steps to where we waited. I watched them. Would they smile at me first? Keep pretending everything was normal? I tried so hard, but I couldn't read their face.

Essie: Hey Ava & Beth! Sorry I've been so bad abt texting. How r u guys?!?!

Ava: Essie! Worst friend EVER!

Beth: Sseerriioouussllyy!!

Essie: Forgive me?

Ava: Always

Beth: Speak for yourself Ava (jk!)

Ava: OK tell us EVERYTHING Em said there was a crush!

Beth: WHOSE PRONOUNS R THEY THEM

Essie: Ollie is nonbinary. Like Morgan in 8th grade (I think Morgan is nonbinary?) Also y r u screaming Beth

Beth: Bc Emily & Ava keep reminding me to use the right pronouns. See Ava I got them right this time r u proud of me

Ava: Love their name Es! My aunt has a dog named Ollie. Tell us everything!

Essie: Sooooo sorry but my dad is totally pestering me right now. Gotta go to grocery with him.

Ava: Just when things were about to get juicy! Text us after?

Essie: K

76 DAYS LEFT

Dad poked his head into my room. I was stretched out on my bed, my Spanish textbook next to me, unopened.

"Hey, Es, I'm running to the mailbox on the corner. Join me? It's a gorgeous night."

"Nah," I replied. "Too lazy."

"Okay. I'll be back in ten."

The front door clicked shut. Even though I hadn't really done anything, I was tired from the day. From my thoughts. About Emily, who had clearly told Beth and Ava what I'd told her not to tell. About Beth and Ava, who were just . . . Beth and Ava. And about Ollie and how we were pretending everything was normal when it definitely wasn't.

I assessed my tally marks and the space surrounding them. If we were repainting in December, we may as well repaint the *entire* wall. I got up and grabbed a pencil from my desk. Carefully, I began to sketch two trees, as high as my head, an empty hammock between them, stars, and a cratered moon overhead. I wanted to re-create the moment in the hammock when we'd *almost* kissed. The moment where Ollie had seemed most completely like just-Ollie. And where, just three days before hiding away in the cocoon on the spinny-spin, I'd felt most like just-me.

"That adds a nice touch," Dad said, startling me. I hadn't even heard him return.

"Geez, Dad," I said, looking from him to the sketch on my wall. "You scared me."

75 DAYS LEFT

After school, I walked to the campus bookstore. The back wall was a patchwork of Post-it notes and pens. Paradise. I took out the two twenties that Dad had agreed to give me and paid $29.99 for a massive pack of colored Sharpies. If I was going to do this, I was going to do it right.

Back home, I sketched hundreds of leaves in varying shades of green and shaded half of one thin tree trunk until my hand ached.

I felt like talking to someone about Ollie and how things were too nice, pretend-normal with them.

And I felt like talking to someone about myself.

I scrolled through old texts with Emily. With Ava and Beth. I even scrolled through the Seventh-Grade Girls Chat. And I scrolled through texts with Mom: *What an exciting adventure; I'm so impressed with your independence. Take advantage of every moment!*

I didn't feel like talking to or texting with anyone from home.

Dad came back from teaching and popped his head into my open doorway. "Nice mural," he commented, pushing his glasses up onto his nose before heading off to bustle around the kitchen and figure out dinner. Not that there was anything *wrong* with Dad, but I definitely didn't want to talk to him about stuff like . . . *this*.

I looked at my texts with Savannah and Luciana, knowing that anything I said to them would go straight to Ollie.

And I scrolled through all of my texts with Ollie.

They were the one I wanted to talk to. But I couldn't do that, and for the first time, I wished I were as bold as Mom thought I was.

Mom **Essie**

Hey Es! How are you kiddo?

Good, you?

Great, tho the house is too quiet with you gone. Also SO busy with this crazy installation. It's nuts but it's going to be awesome. Wish you could see the prototype irl!

Nice

I know we haven't talked.

Sorry I've been so swamped.

Np

Tell me about your adventure.

Have I ever mentioned how much I would have LOVED an opportunity like this when I was your age?! (Kidding—I might have told you)

Yeah you might have mentioned that . . .

You OK? Am I interrupting anything?

No just HW

OK I'll let you go then. Love you!

I wandered into the kitchen, where I slid my phone onto the cluttered counter. Dad was on his laptop in the living room. "Hey," I said to his back.

"Hey!"

"So I was just texting Mom," I said.

He glanced over his shoulder at me. "Yeah? How's everything?"

"Seems good." I looked out the window at the blue siding of the house next door and asked him, "Has she called you recently?"

"No, not for a little while." Labels were so annoying. But so useful. I wanted a label for my parents.

"Are you . . . I mean, is that okay with you?" I pressed.

He closed his laptop and turned to me. "Well, we're both just super busy right now. More important, let's talk dinner. I'm starving, and we've got nothing to eat. Should we try a pizza place that Marianne told me about? It's called Pizza Pizza."

I shrugged. Classic Dad. "Sure."

70 DAYS LEFT

Essie: Hey guys sorry I never got back to you. Been super super busy here but I miss you! What's up???

Ava: Hi!!!

Essie: Hows life and school and everything. What am I missing???

Ava: Its fine, boring, whatever Mr. Andrews quit and we got a new Sci teacher

Essie: Whoa why?!

Ava: Idk. Hows Ollie

Essie: Eh, things are weird. Lets talk abt it later. Tell me more about u. Beth u there?

I have literally never seen u
without ur phone in ur hand
so I know you're reading this

Ava: Lol so true

Essie: BETH!

Ava: We know you're
there!

Essie: OK we'll ignore you
too. Lol. Ava hows the soccer
team doing plz don't win the
1st ever championship
without me

Ava: Decent 4 & 2 but
I'm sure we'll start
sucking again soon lol.
Speaking of which I
have to go my dad is
yelling for me to get my
butt downstairs for
practice

Essie: K have fun!

66 DAYS LEFT

Emily

Essie

Hey, Es!

Hi Em

Just ran into ur mom at grocery!

Lucky you

So whats up?

U there?

Yup

U ok? Are you mad at me or something?

Are you serious?

I'm confused. What's happening?

How could you be confused?! Emily, you told Beth and Ava EXACTLY what I told you not to tell them about me. I reread our texts. I said I'd tell them about Ollie & about ME

Honestly I don't get why it's such a big deal. Nobody cares. That's the point. It's not like we're OLD people who care about that kind of thing

Well I think Beth might care

I doubt it and besides it isn't so simple. Can we just talk about it later? I have to leave for dance

Fine

Fine

64 DAYS LEFT

"I have excellent news!" Ollie announced at the GLOW lunch meeting. "My brother's best friend from high school is Joey Chen. He works for the campus press that's covering the Thankful for Pride march. Joey wanted to help us out, so he submitted our info to ABC News. Now ABC wants to do a thing on us, too!"

Everyone cheered. Grinning, Ollie held my gaze for an extra second. Electricity flickered in my veins.

"I bet we'll get lots more members of GLOW now," they continued. "We can publicize the fact that we're going to be 'famous.' Everyone'll want to join!"

Not that I'd say anything to Ollie about it, but I wondered about the types of people who would join GLOW just because they wanted to be on TV. And wait, Ollie had a brother? What else didn't I know about them?

* * *

"This ABC News thing is *fantastic*," Ollie said as we walked home. Again. "It's going to work in our favor because it will get us new members, plus it will just be awesome. Maybe we should make another announcement Monday morning for the next GLOW meeting . . ."

I looked back and forth between Ollie and the sky; Ollie and the wind-blown branches; Ollie and everything. They talked on and on.

They seemed kind of . . . hyper. Or anxious. Or something. It wasn't that I minded advocate-Ollie, but this was anxious-advocate-Ollie. I wanted to be with just-Ollie. I didn't know where they were, and I missed them.

But if *this* Ollie—this kind of nervous, sort of unrecognizable one—was my only option, I'd settle for them in a heartbeat.

62 DAYS LEFT

I sat on my bedroom floor. My phone, with Emily's blurred face filling the screen, was propped against the leg of my bedside table. "I specifically told you that I would tell Ava and Beth about Ollie and especially that I was wondering what this . . . how to label . . ." I felt stupid. "Why would you tell them when I'd told you not to?"

"I'm sorry, Essie. But it's not like this has been easy for me, either."

"It's not like *what* hasn't been easy for you?"

"I mean, my best friend leaves me for the semester, then tells me over text about all these changes going on with her . . ." She stopped.

"God, Em. I'm still *me*." Saying it made me feel stronger, like light was starting to shine into the cracks of someplace dark.

Emily didn't respond.

"And I told you not to tell," I repeated, envisioning Ava and Beth. Beth, who was clearly weirded out and still hadn't texted me back.

Besides, would who I liked determine some shifting label that I had to advertise? Even though I *was* still curious: If someone liked someone else who was nonbinary, what *would* that person's label be?

"I'm sorry," Emily said, but the way she said it made me feel like all of this was my fault.

"'Kay," I said.

"Bye."

"Bye."

60 DAYS LEFT

Every teacher in the history of forever has insisted that you hang things on school walls with that blue sticky tack. Which is fine, except it doesn't stick. Tuesday afternoon, Ollie, Luciana, Savannah, and I spent an hour hanging posters advertising GLOW *and* the Thankful for Pride news coverage (Ollie's idea). Then we had to rehang them with contraband tape (the horror!) because they'd fallen down.

"OMG!" Ollie yelled dramatically when the four of us turned a corner to find yet another poster with blue sticky tack on its back lying on the ground.

We laughed.

I didn't know if I should stay right by Ollie's side, or give them space. I wanted to stay by their side.

Luciana and Savannah ran off to collect fallen posters. When they disappeared around the corner, Ollie and I sat on the floor in the dim hallway. They pulled the sticky tack off the poster and rolled it between their fingers as I made tape loops to put in its place.

It seemed like they wanted to be with me. Like, right next to me. I could feel our force fields buzzing. But I didn't know what to make of that anymore.

I did know that, by six o'clock, I was starving and tired. My stomach was sore from running through deserted halls after dangling and fallen posters, laughing.

The four of us walked toward campus and decided we should hold all future Thanksgiving Thankful for Pride meetings at Pizza Pizza. "We'd be so productive productive," Ollie joked.

While we were there, I never once thought of Emily, Ava, Beth, Mom, or Dad. Only Ollie, Ollie, Ollie.

58 DAYS LEFT

Ollie had been right. Instead of fourteen people at Thursday's lunch meeting, we filled an entire, long cafeteria table. I looked around it, counting. Thirty-three! A sixth grader named Maria said her parents had a flatbed trailer that we could probably attach to their minivan to make a float. An eighth grader had an aunt who worked at a clothing company and could get us cheap GLOW merch to wear to the march. *March merch*, I thought, just as Ollie said, "Awesome! March merch!" I caught their eye as if to say *That's what I was thinking!*

They grinned at me. Swept their hair out of their eyes.

It was pretty clear that Ollie had been right about this membership thing after all.

They took down notes on their laptop, assigning tasks. They put one group in charge of making a video for the school's website, another in charge of creating more posters.

I felt the energy. It made me feel powerful to be sur-rounded by "hate erasers." Invincible. I'd never really been a part of a group on a mission to do something important before. Maybe it was because I'd been wondering about my own label, but either way, I understood advocate-Ollie a little better.

57 DAYS LEFT

I picked at the paint spatters on the wooden table in art class as Ms. VanVoorhees pulled down the projector screen. Ollie nudged me (*zap*) to show me their fingernail; they'd painted it silver with a paint pen that someone had left out. Outside, a soft rain fell.

"Our next project is going to be to create optical illusions," Ms. VanVoorhees announced. On the screen, a drawing appeared. It was the sketch of the old woman/young woman; I'd seen it before. "What do you see?" Ms. VanVoorhees asked us way too excitedly.

I had to admit that it *was* cool to see how many people—including Ollie—immediately saw the old woman, when I had to search hard for her in the image.

Then she projected a duck/rabbit. "That's so clearly a rabbit," Ollie whispered to me.

I looked from the screen to their eyes. "You're biased," I

told them. "Because of Froggy." I saw it way more clearly as a duck.

Next was a turquoise-and-blue butterfly.

"Whoa," Ollie said, holding their hands up, thumbs pressed together. "I need to paint my hands like that."

I squinted at the illusion. It *was* actually a pair of hands, painted to resemble the wings of a butterfly. Ollie fluttered their fingers. I wanted to squeeze their hands between mine.

I sat on my floor, cross-legged, in front of my partially completed mural, wondering if I could build in an optical illusion. My coffee was still steaming, but I took a sip anyway, burning my lip. If I extended some of the tree branches, the empty space above the hammock could become a heart, with the U-shaped crook of the hammock (sort of) the heart's bottom . . .

My phone buzzed. It was Ollie.

Ollie   **Essie**

Hey Es

                                    Hey Ol

Want to do HW tonight

                              Y!

My dad is having work people
over for dinner—ur house?

My heart rattled as I looked from my wall to my phone.
True, the hammock was still empty, but they would know
exactly what had inspired the scene.

                         How about library

Ok sure no prob. Meet at
upstairs tables at 7?

                         Yup see you soon

53 DAYS LEFT

When I woke up, I drew another tally mark on my wall with my dying black Sharpie and scrolled through my phone. Mom had texted a picture of the first stages of her New York gallery installation, and one of the fancy hotel room she'd be staying in for the next two weeks.

Cool, I replied.

I hadn't texted with Emily, Ava, or Beth in what felt like forever, and I already knew everything would be awkward when I returned home for Thanksgiving break, and then for good in December. It dawned on me that it would have been better if Mom and Dad had sent me to a new school in a new town for a full year. I mean, that way, at least I could have had a chance to settle in.

After school, I walked through rain puddles toward the bookstore. My socks were soaked by the time I arrived.

Thankfully, there were loose Sharpies for sale, so I could replenish my supply of blacks, browns, and greens.

Despite my wet feet, I took the long way home. I thought of Ollie as I walked, how it had been hard to focus on homework at the library with our force fields pulling together like magnets. How our knees had touched as I'd leaned over to look at their laptop. How I was pretty sure that things between us were, at least, *on the way* to returning to how they'd been before. And how I hoped they'd hurry up. Because in two months, I'd be gone.

I peered into the window of a coffeehouse as I passed by, but then I stopped. Through the glass, distorted by my reflection, was Dad. And across from him, laughing, hands wrapped around a mug, was a woman.

52 DAYS LEFT

I stirred a spoonful of sugar into my coffee as Dad got dressed in his bedroom. I felt annoyed—no, *angry*—at everything. Not just with Dad and that woman in the coffee shop; it was more than that. First, Mom and Dad had made me come to North Carolina *against my will*. Now I didn't really want to leave, but I'd have to. What did everything mean? I wanted words—for all of it. For Mom and Dad. For Ollie. For me. Names, labels—they would help me understand what was going on.

I stood in front of my coffee mug to block it from Dad's view when he came out of the bedroom. "Okay!" he said, clapping his hands together. "Almost ready to head out?"

"Who was that woman you were having coffee with yesterday?" I asked him.

He looked confused. "What were you doing all the way on Fifth Street?"

"Does that matter?" I was sick of being treated like a totally dependent child by one parent and a completely independent woman by the other.

"No, I suppose it doesn't. I was just curious." He ran his fingers through his still-damp, thinning hair. "Lillian is one of my teaching assistants. She's a grad student. We were going over her course material for second semester. She's never been an assistant before, and she was nervous."

I nodded, not knowing what to think. I mean, the idea of Dad cheating on Mom *was* pretty outrageous. I couldn't exactly imagine him showing up for a secret date in his pleated khaki pants and a sweater vest.

"Ready to head out?" he asked again.

I nodded. "Ready."

Later that afternoon, in art, we brainstormed ideas for our own optical illusions. Even though I couldn't imagine Dad on a date, it was hard to stop thinking about him and the teaching assistant. The way he looked with her—interested, happy—that's how I *wished* he looked when he was with Mom. And how I wished Mom looked when she was with him.

I tried to be rational. It *was* probably nothing to worry about. If I drew the scene through the coffeehouse window, maybe one person would see Dad laughing with a pretty woman—her hands clasping a steaming mug, her silent laugh—because he was cheating on Mom, while another person would see something else entirely. Old woman, young woman. Duck, rabbit. Butterfly, hands.

49 DAYS LEFT

I sat across from Dad awkwardly at Siri's Indian Cuisine. I was eager to finish and get to Savannah's for Halloween with her and Luciana. And Ollie.

Dad worked his way through his curry, oblivious. When he finally finished and paid in slow motion, he took our bag of leftovers and walked me across campus—bustling with kids and college students, all out for Halloween.

Savannah answered the door quickly when I rang the bell. "Oh, thank goodness it's not another trick-or-treater. We just ran out of candy, and my mom had to go buy more."

"Already?" I asked, waving goodbye to Dad.

"Halloween is a *thing* here," she replied.

Inside, Ollie and Luciana sat atop the kitchen island, eating homemade rice crispy treats out of a pan. Savannah introduced me to her dad and little sister, Lindsay, who were preparing to head out.

"Peanut butter chip rice crispy treat?" Ollie asked, holding one out to me.

"The Ollie special," Luciana added.

"Sure." I pulled it off their hand, feigning cool as I hopped onto the countertop next to them.

"Savannah, you might be too old to trick-or-treat this year, but come get in a picture with your sister," Savannah's dad said, lowering Lindsay's werewolf mask over her eyes.

Luciana jumped down. "I'll take one of the three of you," she offered. Ollie and I watched as Savannah, Lindsay, and her dad posed for Luciana in front of the fireplace.

"Werewolves creep me out," I admitted to Ollie. "Big-time."

They laughed. "For real? I love Halloween. This is the first year I haven't dressed up and gone trick-or-treating."

"Seriously? I kind of hate it. What do you love about it?"

"Nobody knows who you are."

"But everyone loves you."

"It's not that—it's just that it doesn't matter who you are because everyone can be anyone."

"That seems scary to me," I told them. "Being anonymous."

"Yeah. But every once in a while, it's kind of awesome."

47 DAYS LEFT

Ollie's mom had invited me and Dad over for dinner. Dad, who never would have thought to bring something to a guest's house back home, had picked up a plant with orange flowers at the farmer's market earlier that day. When we arrived at Ollie's house, he shook hands with Adam, Ollie's dad, and handed the plant to Marianne.

"How beautiful," she said, lifting it out of its plastic and placing it carefully on the dining table.

"It's the least I could do. You've been so helpful with all of your advice," Dad replied.

I looked at Ollie. *The least he could do? All of* what *advice?* But they just shrugged and handed me a bowl of veggie chili, their dad's specialty.

We settled around the table. Ollie took a bite of cornbread and nudged me. "A smile?" they asked me, turning it over. "Or a bridge?"

I laughed. Across the room, Froggy thumped in her cage. "I think your duck wants some alfalfa," I told them.

For a second, Dad and Ollie's parents looked at us like we were nuts, but they jumped easily into conversation about the upcoming weeklong Thanksgiving break. Marianne wiped a crumb off Adam's lip. He kissed her head on the way to the kitchen for another spoon. I turned my attention back to Ollie until something Dad said caught my ear: "Her teachers are fine with her missing school on the Friday before the break."

I interrupted, suddenly not interested in being polite, despite the fact that we were with guests. "What?"

Dad turned to me. "Oh, you don't mind, do you? I emailed your teachers and they're fine with you missing November 20. That will give you an extra—"

"You emailed my teachers? What do you think I am, a baby? And how about asking me? How do you even know that I *want* to go home early?"

"Honey," Dad said, looking embarrassed, "let's discuss it later."

I looked from him to Ollie. Leaving a day early for an already weeklong Thanksgiving break meant less time with Ollie. Which was the exact opposite of what I wanted.

46 DAYS LEFT

The next morning, I woke up to a text from Ollie: *Hey Es.*

Essie   **Ollie**

Hey Ol

> Sorry parents suck so bad.
> Why don't u want to go
> home?

I don't know how to
explain it

> I get that. Like there aren't
> the right words or enough
> words

Yeah exactly

> Do u want to talk about it?

Eh not really

Ok want me to distract u with something?

Yes!

What do you think of a poster contest for GLOW and the winner gets their entry blown up to poster size and copied and passed out to participants at the march. Ms Rose will b the judge. Deadline in like a week or 2

Sweet!

☺ Did u finish that stupid English essay last night?

I wish

Are you doing anything tonight?

Finishing that stupid English essay

Same

Want to work on it together?

Definitely!

Cool. Ur house ok?

Sure

44 DAYS LEFT

I woke up before my alarm. In the kitchen, the automatic start on the coffeemaker flipped on. When it stopped gurgling, I got out of bed. The kitchen was dark; Dad was still asleep.

I brought my coffee back into my bedroom and sat on the floor in front of my mural. I'd already extended the branches from the trees on my bedroom wall so the empty space between them created the top of a heart. I'd done my best to make the leaves North Carolina–fall-like. The scene was browns, yellows, greens, starlight. But the hammock was still a sharply curved, penciled line.

I scrolled through my phone. I'd gotten another picture from Mom, this one of her and a man in an Xavier's Gallery shirt, standing together in front of her partially completed installation. *I was telling everyone at the gallery how proud I am of you!* she'd written. I zoomed in on the man's handsome face, and then on the barely existent space between their shoulders.

Reluctantly, I "liked" the picture, brought my coffee into the bathroom, and started the shower.

Later that day, in art, I leaned over Ollie's laptop to see their optical illusion. It was a variation on Rubin's Vase, the illusion that looked either like two profiles staring at each other or like a vase, depending on how you saw it. They were doing it with Photoshop, which, given their drawing abilities, was a good idea. "I'm so turning this into a Thankful for Pride poster contest entry," they said, blending the colors in the vase (or the space) into a rainbow.

"That's a perfect idea," I told them.

"This is your friendly reminder that the deadline to email your entry is just eight days away!" They wiggled their eyebrows at me. "Hey, Ms. Rose had a great idea," they went on. "She's not going to announce the winner ahead of time; we'll arrive at the march and have to look at the posters to find out who won!"

I thought of the mural on my wall. It would make a good poster contest entry, too. If I wanted to, I could write GLOW in the heart and send a picture of it to Ms. Rose.

If I was brave enough to take a risk like that.

41 DAYS LEFT

Froggy sat in the middle of the coffee table twitching her nose as Savannah, Luciana, and I took turns feeding her strands of alfalfa.

"Best day ever to be a duck," Ollie said.

I laughed as Luciana and Savannah rolled their eyes.

"You guys need to let it go with the ducks and rabbits," Luciana told us.

"And the old women and young women . . . ," Savannah added.

"Don't forget the butterflies and the hands," Luciana chimed in, laughing.

"You're both just jealous that you don't have Ms. VanVoorhees for art," Ollie told them. "You know her class is a thousand times better than Mr. Hoffman's. Hey, is everyone done with their poster contest entries?"

"Almost," Luciana said, holding up her right hand dramatically. "Look at this blister I gave myself from the *artwork* that I created last night."

"Don't be a drama queen," Savannah told her, batting her hand away.

Ollie raised their eyebrows at me. "How about you?" they asked.

I thought of the almost-finished heart on my wall. "No comment," I replied.

I was feeling uneasy—about the mural on my wall that I knew I should photograph and submit to Ms. Rose for Ollie's contest; about the fact that, once I returned from Thanksgiving break, I'd only have three more weeks in North Carolina; and about going home for break the following week, in general.

I imagined my inner Essie, freed from its cocoon, like a butterfly, and how it would feel to tell Mom to start acting like an *actual* mom; to make Emily, Ava, and Beth understand that me and Ollie, well, that was just about me loving . . . liking . . . okay, loving them.

I stayed up way too late doing homework and then finishing the mural. Not to brag, but it was pretty good. Ollie's eyes were black-rimmed blue. From across my room, the heart stood out. It was a *reverse* heart—a heart that had been formed by erasing things that had been in the way. When you shifted your focus, everything else came into view.

I wrote *GLOW* inside the heart, took a picture of it, and, before I could think too hard, emailed the entry to Ms. Rose.

36 DAYS LEFT

The next morning, Dad poked his head into my room before school. "Whoa, you're finished," he said, evaluating the wall.

I tried putting myself into his shoes and wondered how uncomfortable it made him to see what he saw: a very, very gigantic drawing on a very, very rented wall. "Hey, Dad."

He came in. "This is really quite good." He ran his fingers over the trees, my red sandals, Ollie's black Converse, my navy sweatshirt with *LOVE* written across the front of it . . . "Are these two people anyone in particular?"

"Eh, not really," I lied.

He looked from me to the wall, and I wondered if he believed me.

Later that day, in art, Ollie and I leaned over our projects. Mine was a "box-sphere illusion." There was a 3-D cube with a little sphere next to it. Or, inside of it, depending on how you saw it. Repeating words comprised the black lines of the cube: *Saint Louis, Marriage, Family, Childhood.*

The circle was a sketch of my face, which, if you looked at it one way, would be inside the box. But then if you squinted slightly, looked at it differently, it would be floating just outside it, peering in.

My mind kept drifting to home. It was like I actually *was* the head in my optical illusion: part of the time I felt totally separate from life in Saint Louis, but then when I'd think of things differently, I'd be right back there in my mind.

I was nervous. I knew when I went home, I'd have to say something to Emily. To Ava and Beth. Maybe even to Mom. I decided to get one conversation out of the way.

Essie **Emily**

Hey Em. Long time no talk. I've been thinking a lot about why it bothered me so much that you told Ava and Beth what

I was thinking about.
I told u not to so that
was NOT cool but it's
also something about
labels and how they're
so annoying but also so
useful. But so annoying.
Like does it matter what
my label is

I didn't wait 8 hours to text
back because I'm mad. I was
just trying to think. And also,
you're right I shouldn't have told
them when you told me not to.
That was really stupid of me. It
has really sucked for me since
you left and especially now that
you're so settled there. It seems
like you've been gone forever.
Maybe I was trying to get closer
to A & B coz they're like a pair
and you were my pair. My labels =
awful friend, desperate, stupid.

Forgive me?

Forgiven.

32 DAYS LEFT

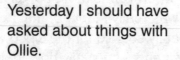

Emily

Essie

Yesterday I should have asked about things with Ollie.

Things are getting back to good

Have u asked them why things got weird?

No!!!!

Why? Remember you said u wanted to put urself out there more and stuff

Ya u have reminded me of that

Have I?

Yes and I dunno why I
didn't ask. Cause I kinda
love them?

(Kidding)

(Not kidding)

Lol but seriously I don't
get it

Me either weirdest best
crush I've ever had.

My dad is yelling at
me to put phone away.
Indian food tuesday. We
aren't even supposed
to go on tuesdays. Save
meeeee. . . . .

Good luck!!

31 DAYS LEFT

Essie

Emily

Hey

Hey!

Yesterday I should have asked about things with you

You there?

Yeah. Sorry. Things are just ok

☹ Why?

Because everything sucks when your best friend moves. So yeah

☹

It's been bad. I'm totally
a 3rd wheel. I feel like
such a loser

Why didn't u tell me
sooner

It would have made it
real

You there?

Yeah just thinking

About?

Dunno, labels, words. How
things become real

When you get back will
everything be like when
we were in 6th grade
again?

Maybe . . .

Yeah . . .

30 DAYS LEFT

"Es?" Dad asked, poking his head into my bedroom. I was piling clothes into my purple suitcase.

"Yeah?"

"We'll leave tomorrow morning for the airport at around eight, okay?"

"Sure," I said, dreading the thought of flying. And of being home.

"And then," he continued nervously, "I'll spend the night and fly back the next morning."

I closed my suitcase and faced him. "You're not staying for Thanksgiving?"

"I have so much work to get done here . . ." He paused.

I wanted to yell at him for all the words he was leaving unspoken, but it dawned on me that I couldn't do that when there was so much that I wasn't saying myself.

So I focused on not crying and asked him: "Are you and Mom getting divorced? I want you to tell me."

"Divorced?" He looked frozen.

"I'm not a baby, Dad," I went on, hoping he wouldn't notice that I was trying to fight back tears.

He sighed. "I know."

"So?"

He sat down on my bed and rubbed his wrinkled forehead with his palms. "I don't know, hon. The visiting professorship didn't just 'come up.' Obviously. I applied for it. Mom and I needed time apart." I thought again of Dad and his teaching assistant in the coffeehouse. And of the very small space between Mom and the man in the Xavier's shirt.

"I figured," I said, sitting at my desk pretending to put all my Sharpies back in order so Dad wouldn't see my face. Deep down, I *had* known, which didn't explain my feelings. Because even though I'd seen it coming, I didn't *want* Mom and Dad to need "time apart." I wanted them to love each other.

And because maybe Mom had wanted time apart from *me*, too.

29 DAYS LEFT

Mom was waiting for me and Dad in the passenger pickup line at the airport. When we got to the car, she jumped out and hugged me as Dad arranged our suitcases in the trunk. "Thank goodness you don't look any different," she said, smoothing my hair. "I had a vision that you'd come back home totally grown up!"

"You did?" I asked, getting into the backseat. It wasn't a very *my* mom-like thing to say.

I paid specific attention to the fact that she and Dad barely acknowledged each other, which, honestly, wasn't so different from the way things had always been.

"What ended up happening with the plumbers?" Dad asked as Mom pulled onto the street. "Watch that car," he directed as she changed lanes.

"I got it, Walt," she snapped. Then she launched into an

explanation about the leaking pipe in the kitchen. "I got two quotes. The third guy never showed."

I listened to them talk. Their conversation was like their conversations had been my entire life: polite most of the time, snippy some of the time. Had they ever felt the zaps when they were together the way I did when I was with Ollie? I couldn't imagine it.

When we got home, I rolled my suitcase toward the stairs, down the red rug that I'd walked across who knows how many times but that somehow I'd forgotten since being away. Walking into my room felt even stranger. The light-blue carpet, the quilt on my bed—everything made me think of who I'd been before I'd gone to North Carolina. Even though only three months had passed, I felt like a different person. Downstairs, Mom and Dad were poking around under the kitchen sink, talking about the pipe. I took out my phone and texted Emily.

Essie **Emily**

I'm home! What r u doing today

Hi!!!!!! Ugh family time can't hang out till

tomorrow my parents r
being annoying about it
☹ Ping pong tournament
in basement. Help

Haha! Are you at least
winning

Of course not

Can't wait to see you!
My dad is leaving in the
morning

Really??? Why??

Because my parents
hate each other?

Kidding

Not kidding

OK we need to
discuss. Parents
are making me put
away my phone ☹

K talk to u tomorrow

Family time. I wandered downstairs to the kitchen. Dad
was standing up, closing the cabinet door under the sink,
and wiping his damp hands on his jeans. Mom was taking a
head of lettuce out of the fridge. Family time in this house
meant three people coexisting.

28 DAYS LEFT

On Saturday morning, I woke up early. My room didn't feel like *my room*. I missed my mural. And I missed knowing that Ollie was just four blocks away. I texted Emily.

Essie **Emily**

U r prob sleeping lmk when ur up! My house is depressing. What do u wanna do today?

I crept downstairs quietly but startled when I got to the bottom of the stairs. Dad was asleep, mouth open, snoring, on the couch. The sight of him there made tears spring to my eyes. It felt like a symbol of the fact that everything was about to change. I tiptoed around him into the kitchen to make the coffee. As I took out a mug, my phone dinged.

Essie **Emily**

> My parents r dragging us to a new brunch place that they LOVE

> So come over at like 1:00?
> Cant wait to see u!

Have fun and hurry I have nothing to do!

> Hang with ur mom?

Yeah right

> Yeah I guess I can't really see that

Seriously

> Ur dad still going back today?

Yup. This is weird

> IKR. Sorry. Lets discuss this afternoon

Definitely

Mom dropped me off at Emily's after we took Dad to the airport.

"Oh my God, you're taller," I told Emily when she opened the front door and threw her arms around me.

"Essie!" her mom called out, coming down the stairs. "We've missed you!" She hugged me, too.

Then Emily's little brother and dad hugged me, and all of that hugging made me . . . sad. Sad that my family sucked in comparison.

"Come to my room," Emily said, dragging me upstairs. "Tell me everything."

"I think they're getting divorced," I told her, flopping onto her bed. Strangely, I felt numb about it, like someone else was telling her about *their* family.

"Are you kidding me?" she asked.

"Nope."

"Are you shocked?"

"I shouldn't be, but for some reason I am."

"I totally get that," she'd said. "I mean, do you know for sure?"

"Not really. My dad said they 'needed time apart.'"

"Ask your mom?"

"My mom . . . Why is my mom so *aloof*?"

"Ask her?"

"For real?"

"Remember you were saying you'd been wanting to put yourself out there more?"

"I remember."

27 DAYS LEFT

Rain pounded on my window on Sunday morning. The house felt so empty as I walked downstairs that I wondered if Mom had gone out to do errands without telling me. All the lights were off and rain gusted against the roof. I finally found her in her studio, where she sat, back to me, hunched over a model of what was most likely her next project. It was *definitely* small enough to have been easily moved to North Carolina. "Hey," I said.

She turned around. "Hey, hon! How'd you sleep?" she asked, putting down her paintbrush.

"Fine."

She nodded. "What's your plan today? Isn't it gross out? Are you hanging out with friends later? Can I give you a ride anywhere?"

I thought of the spinny-spin, because listening to her questions made me remember my cocoon. I'd wrapped myself inside it because I'd felt insecure, and I felt insecure because of her. Because of *this*.

"Do you even want to spend time with me?" I definitely hadn't *meant* to yell it or to start crying, but once I did, the cocoon started to crack and everything I'd been feeling for so long began leaking out.

She looked stunned. "Of course I do."

"Well, it sure doesn't seem like it."

"When I was your age, I would have done anything to have just had the freedom to—"

"*I'm not you!*" I yelled at her.

"Of course you're not," she said quickly, taken aback.

"So maybe I want the type of mother who actually *wants to be* with her daughter. And what's going on with you and Dad, anyway? I'm sick of all these vague answers like 'we need time apart' and 'I have lots of work to do in North Carolina.' Are you getting divorced? If I'm supposed to be so 'independent,' why haven't you told me what's happening?"

Mom nodded slowly. It looked like she was going to cry, too, but I didn't feel bad for her.

"Okay," she finally said. "Let's talk."

25 DAYS LEFT

I lay on my bed, staring at my mural-less wall. The sun was barely up, but I'd been awake forever.

"You know none of this is your fault," Mom had started when I'd planted myself on her studio floor.

I'd rolled my eyes. "Come on, Mom," I'd told her. "Don't be such a cliché."

She'd smiled a little, joined me on the rug, and looked up at the ceiling. "You seem so much older," she finally said, wiping her eyes.

Seeing her cry had made my eyes well up even more.

"Okay," she had said, as if to steady herself. "So your dad and I have probably never been a good fit. There's never really been—"

"Electricity? Zaps?"

She'd looked at me like she was wondering who I was. "Yeah," she'd said. "So we were basically just moving forward together, but not together, until your dad suggested that maybe we weren't being fair." She grabbed a tissue from her desk and blew her nose. "To ourselves."

I was so shocked that, for a second, I felt dizzy. "*Dad? Dad was the one who wanted this?*"

She wadded up her used tissue. "Yeah," she finally said. "But everything's going to be friendly," she went on, after a pause. "Low drama."

"Where . . . Who's going to live where? What's going to happen? I mean, am I—"

"Dad's planning to extend his stay at the university. They want him to teach again next term."

I nodded.

"You and I will be here. My travel schedule is light next semester. After that, we'll figure it out. Maybe Dad will rent a place nearby . . . We'll have to see. It's going to be okay," Mom said, like she was trying to convince both herself and me. "Everything is going to work out." She took a deliberate breath. "Is there anything you want to ask me? Anything I've left out?"

I shook my head.

"Okay. So it's going to be disgusting all day. Let's do something together. What do you say? Museum?"

She had a streak of black paint in her messy hair and her eyes were red and puffy.

"Yeah," I told her. "Good idea."

24 DAYS LEFT

The day before Thanksgiving, the rain finally stopped. Emily, Ava, Beth, and I had met at Starbucks in the morning. Now we sat on my bedroom floor.

"Just like old times!" Ava said, tossing my sequined, poop-shaped pillow into the air.

Emily caught it. "Why do you still have this sparkly poop pillow?" she asked me, laughing.

"Um, because you gave it to me two years ago for my birthday?"

"It's so immature," Emily said. "What was I thinking?"

I laughed, too, remembering how cool it had seemed at the time. "I have no idea."

"Okay," Beth announced. "Time for Essie to spill everything about Ollie. I didn't want to bring it up in Starbucks."

Why not? I wondered. But I told her, Ava, and Emily everything anyway, from a recap of the bad kiss to the way that things seemed to be getting better.

"Okay, wait," Beth said as soon as I'd finished.

Emily gave me a look and Ava watched Beth nervously, as if she was worried about where this was going.

"I seriously don't understand. This whole nonbinary thing just seems very vague. Like, I'm a girl, because that's how I was born, right? I'm not 'girly.' I don't wear skirts or dresses. But that doesn't make *me* identify as nonbinary. It doesn't make sense."

Everything about Beth's comment felt wrong, but I didn't know how to respond. How was I supposed to explain Ollie's gender to someone who didn't want to understand it? "Ollie doesn't '*identify* as nonbinary,'" I finally said. "Ollie *is* nonbinary." It was a fraction of what I wanted to say, but it was all that I could get out.

"So does this make you gay? Not that I'd care if you were."

I rolled my eyes and shot Emily an *I told you so* look. "It *seems* like you'd care," I told her.

"I wouldn't," Beth answered quickly. "I'm just curious."

Ava jumped in. "Beth, isn't your dad getting us now? It's noon."

Beth glanced at the time on her phone. "Yeah, I guess he is."

"Walk us out?" Ava asked me and Emily, getting up. *I'll text you*, she mouthed to me as we walked downstairs, and I nodded, frozen, not knowing what to think.

23 DAYS LEFT

"Hey, Es," Mom said as I wandered into the kitchen.

"This feels like the most depressing Thanksgiving ever," I told her, sitting down at the table. It was only four o'clock and already the sun was setting. Dad had texted earlier to check in. Apparently, at the last minute, he had been invited to have Thanksgiving dinner with the pretty teaching assistant and her family. I had no idea what to think of that. Mom and I would be leaving soon. Every Thanksgiving, we went to her old college friend's house, along with about forty other people—none of whom were remotely fun to talk to.

Mom sighed. "I know. It's the worst."

"I don't even like turkey," I told her.

"I could take it or leave it." The clock ticked on the wall. "We could do something else," she finally said, smiling a little.

"Like what?" I asked. "Everything's closed. And besides, Holly's expecting us."

She grabbed her phone to look something up. "Okay," she finally said, grinning mischievously. "Here's our plan: You have an *awful* cold. Unfortunately, you're just not up for dinner at Holly's. And I certainly wouldn't want you to infect anyone with your cooties."

"You're kidding, right?"

"Target," she went on. "Slushies for dinner. Then a movie."

"Are you serious?" I asked.

She *looked* serious. And kind of sad. This time, I felt sorry for her. "I am," she said.

Target was packed with Black Friday shoppers, but thankfully the café at the front of the store was empty. We mixed together all the slushy flavors and sat on the tall stools at the closed Starbucks.

"I'm sorry, Es," Mom said. "About all of this. It's just that I'd never have imagined you *wanting* to do this kind of thing with me. When I was your age . . ."

I shot her a look.

"When I was your age, I was really different from how you are now," she finished.

I pulled out my phone and googled *optical illusions*. "Mom?" I asked, taking a slurp of my slushy and showing her the phone. "Does this look like a duck or a rabbit to you?"

We scrolled through the illusions. I told her about Ollie—how I felt when I was with them—and she told me she was proud of me for being me. Outside, thunder rumbled. Raindrops fell through passing headlights. But was it rain? Or stars? Fireworks, or fairy dust? Maybe everything was also something else.

Hey Essie

Hey Ava

Waz up

Nothing u?

I'm sorry about Beth ☹

Not ur fault

I know but still

Yeah

I talked to my aunt & her wife abt it I hope u don't mind

I don't mind

They're really smart about stuff

Nice

So I wanted 2 tell u that I'm gonna work on Beth like teach her y she is being an idiot abt this. So u don't have to.

Rly?

Is that ok

Yeah it's a relief cause I don't feel like dealing

Totally. Stay tuned k? xoxo

Xoxo

20 DAYS LEFT

Mom parked the car in short-term parking and walked me inside the airport, where we got everything situated for me to fly as an "unaccompanied minor."

"Isn't this exciting?" she asked, handing me the paperwork. I looked at her skeptically and she scrunched her nose. "I'm sorry," she said. "Can I try again? How do you feel about flying alone?"

"I hate flying," I told her. "And I'm sure I'll hate flying alone even more."

She nodded and hugged me. "Sorry, Es," she said. Then she put her arm around me and walked me to the plane. "Text me as soon as you land?" she asked when it was time to board.

"'Kay."

"You know, you're growing up."

"It happens," I told her.

"What I meant to say is that I'm *proud* of the *way* you're growing up. I never was able to tell anyone what I needed when I was your age."

I thought about what Mom said, and, when I got on the plane, I texted Ollie.

Essie

Hey o!

    Hi!!!!!

I'm taking off soon

    YAY!

I'm excited to see u

    Me too

Be home soon

    I'll be here

19 DAYS LEFT

Even though I couldn't wait to see Ollie, part of me was stuck in my head. I couldn't stop thinking of Dad, sleeping on the couch that first night; my bedroom in Saint Louis with its mural-less wall; Beth's face as she'd asked me about Ollie and about myself; multicolored slushies; all the texts I'd gotten since I'd landed. From Mom.

Knowing that Mom and Dad were getting divorced kind of made me feel like throwing up, but at least it was good to know what was happening. I felt better. Calmer. About everything and everyone.

Except for Dad.

I couldn't quite wrap my brain around him. I'd studied him from the passenger seat as we'd driven home from the airport. His glasses had been crooked, like always. He probably hadn't trimmed his ear hair in a million years. How could *he* have been the one to instigate the divorce?

Maybe it wasn't all that different from the way I had an inner Essie, and Ollie had an inner Ollie. Maybe it was about the way that everyone has so many layers. And an idea came to me. One that made me feel like my inner Essie was stepping out completely from a dark enclosure.

17 DAYS LEFT

One *really* good thing about going home for Thanksgiving had been forgetting about the fact that I'd submitted a picture of my mural to the poster contest. Now that I was back, Ollie reminded me constantly.

"Two days until the event!" they announced to all the members when GLOW met in the gym after school. "I'm so excited to see who won the poster contest!"

If I won the poster contest, Ollie would know exactly how I felt about them. It would be like reaching my hand for Ollie's and hoping that they would take it.

And what if they didn't?

Ollie made a big show of opening a plastic bag filled with T-shirts. They were gray with rainbow hearts and GLOW written on the front. The backs read, WE ARE HATE ERASERS.

Maria's mom had towed their flatbed trailer to the gym's side door so we could decorate it. We split into pairs and got to work. Ollie and I lined the backs of signs and posters with loops of duct tape, and Luciana and Savannah ran them outside one by one and pressed them to the sides of the flatbed.

Halfway through, we took a break. Ollie reached their hand toward my face. The force field around them was fully charged. "Hey, you have duct tape in your hair," they told me, touching it. Their force field broke. But only for a second. To let me in.

I smiled at them, their hand still in my hair. "Rabbit tape?" I asked.

16 DAYS LEFT

Essie

Mom

Hey mom u there

Hi!

How r u

Doing ok. How about you?

Doing ok

How is it being back?

It's good being back

I'm glad for you/sad for me. I miss you!

♥

What's new in NC?

Nothing

Actually something

Im confused

Why?

I made a mural

Dad told me. He said it's amazing.

He did? Well by making the mural I put myself out there and I kinda maybe but not rly wanna take it back but I can't

Hmm. Well, is the part of yourself that you revealed genuine?

Yeah

Then I tend to think you'll be OK.I trust you.

Thanks

Anytime.

15 DAYS LEFT

I was jittery on the day of the Thankful for Pride march. But not good jittery. At lunchtime, I poked at my food as Ollie talked excitedly about the news crew, the publicity, the exposure. "Hey, you okay?" they finally asked.

I shrugged, not knowing what to say. *I'm kind of regretting my poster contest entry* didn't seem like an option. Especially given the fact that, if I'd actually won, the posters would have been created days ago. There was definitely no going back.

After school, Ollie and I each headed home to change before meeting the rest of GLOW on campus. In my bedroom, I stood in front of my mural, in front of my heart. *What if Ollie doesn't like me the way I like them?* I thought.

It was three twenty. I put on my GLOW shirt. Brushed my hair. Sat on my bed. Looked at my tally marks. Imagined Ollie potentially seeing my mural plastered across who knows how many posters.

I thought of Mom. How she had been so confident that I had been fine without her.

It was three forty. Time to leave. I stood up. Sat back down. My drawing of Ollie was so clearly Ollie. The drawing of me, so clearly me.

It was four o'clock. My phone buzzed. I put it on silent and shoved it in my desk drawer.

Five o'clock. I turned on the TV. Pulled out my homework.

Six o'clock. GLOW would be starting their march around campus.

Eight o'clock. Dad came home. Poked his head into my bedroom, oblivious to the march. "Have you eaten?" he asked.

"Yup," I lied.

Ten o'clock. I stared up at my ceiling in the dark.

14 DAYS LEFT

Early the next morning, the doorbell rang. I sat up in bed. My bedroom was gray in the misty light. I put on my sweatshirt and went to the door.

Ollie stood on the front porch, hands tucked in their coat pockets. The wind blew their hair sideways. Their face looked hard. I opened my mouth and then closed it.

"You won," they said.

I nodded, wanting to be able to say so many things.

"How could you have just ditched me like that?" they went on.

I'd never seen Ollie like this.

"Was your poster why you didn't . . . I mean, you *knew* how important the march was to me," they went on. "We worked so hard on everything. How could you have just not come? I texted you, like, a thousand times." Their eyes glistened as if they were trying not to cry. "Was it because of the poster?" they asked. "It was good. Was it us? It was us, wasn't it?"

I didn't *want* to be so stuck and silent. Not with Ollie standing right in front of me. I couldn't find the words that I needed, so I reached my hand for theirs.

13 DAYS LEFT

It was suddenly as if time were moving in fast-forward. Ollie came over and we lay down on my floor, beneath the heart. "Ollie?" I asked, looking at the two of us in my mural. "Was it totally obvious to everyone?"

"Was what obvious?" they joked.

"Shut up." I smacked their arm. Zaps flickered.

"Sorry. No, just to Luciana and Savannah. They know everything, anyway." They nudged me. "You've got guts."

I took a breath. "I'm so sorry," I told them again. "I just couldn't bear to see your reaction. To my . . ." I couldn't finish the sentence, so Ollie finished it for me.

"To your heart?" they asked.

12 DAYS LEFT

I couldn't stop thinking about the fact that Ollie thought I wasn't a wimp. Because if I *actually* had guts, I'd say . . .

1. Do you feel zaps when you're with me? I mean, I *feel* like you do, but
2. When we kissed, you didn't, right?
3. Because I didn't either. Why?
4. And, I want to kiss you again, because this time, I'm sure we'll feel them.

After school, Ollie and I sat on my front porch steps even though it was cold—like actual, winter cold. According to weather.com, a snowstorm was coming.

"Get ready to see all of North Carolina shut down," Ollie joked. "We'll probably have a snow day tomorrow."

I grabbed their phone from them to look at the weather report. "It's only supposed to snow two inches!" I said.

"Just watch," they told me, grinning.

11 DAYS LEFT

Sure enough, the next morning the call came that school was canceled. Dad came in to tell me the news.

"I can't believe they're closing school for two inches!" I said, looking out the window.

He laughed. "I know. *Southern snowstorms.* Coffee's—" He cut himself off, still smiling slightly. "I'm going to get my coffee." Then he added, "There's a new hazelnut coffee creamer in the fridge that I thought we should try," before disappearing into the kitchen.

I walked to Ollie's that afternoon to "play in the snow." There was only half an inch left by one o'clock, but still, playing outside was like being a kid. It was like labels didn't matter—or at least, didn't matter *as much*. I felt like the energy between Ollie and me was just an indication of having fun, not something that threatened to electrocute the world as I spilled a slushy "snowball" into their outstretched hand.

Next door, the front door opened and two adults emerged.

"I haven't introduced you to Annabella and Damien yet, have I?"

"Nope," I said.

"I'm Annabella's mini me," Ollie explained, waving.

Annabella wore a red coat and had long blond hair that was pulled into a low ponytail. Damien was bald with a red beard and lots of earrings.

"Annabella is nonbinary, pan . . . ," Ollie went on.

Pan? I thought of fried eggs and half-goats. Ollie read my mind as they dragged me across the lawn to introduce us.

"It means you could be attracted to anyone on the gender spectrum."

"Oh," I said, relieved. Could it really be so simple that *that* was my label? "Cool."

10 DAYS LEFT

Dad, Marianne, Lillian-the-teaching-assistant, and another professor were having a work dinner, so Ollie's dad was taking Ollie and me to dinner at Satter's Platters, which, apparently, had *the best guac in the universe*. I didn't understand the hype over avocados, but whatever.

"Lady and gentlemen, your menus," the waiter said, handing them to us and taking our drink orders (root beers all around).

Ollie subtly rolled their eyes at me in response to the waiter's greeting, and then leaned over and pointed to the roast duck on my menu. "Roast rabbit?" they asked, giggling.

"Oh, did you remember to feed your duck before we left?" I asked, cracking up.

Their dad tried not to smile.

I wondered how it felt to be Ollie. When I saw someone, I always noted their gender first. How would it feel to not be a "boy" or "girl"? I stood in their shoes (black Converse high-tops—so Ollie). Would I feel angry? Misunderstood? Better-than? Or just aware—always aware?

9 DAYS LEFT

Thursday night, Ollie knocked on the front door after dinner, a plastic bag and flashlight in hand.

"What is—" I started to ask, but they held up their hand.

"Patience, young Jedi."

In my bedroom, they emptied a pile of glow-in-the-dark stars and a moon from the bag. "I picked these off my ceiling. You're welcome," they said, smiling. "I know you're leaving soon, but I still wanted you to have them." Then, standing on my desk chair, they added the stars to the inside of my heart and hung the moon. When they shone the flashlight onto the mural and turned off the light, the wall literally glowed.

"That's so awesome," I said, taking Ollie's hand. I wanted to say so many things, but all I could do was feel the energy rocketing through my body. "Thank you."

8 DAYS LEFT

"I have a department event tonight," Dad told me after school on Friday. "Sorry, hon. Can we have Indian-food Friday on Saturday?"

"Dad?"

"Yeah?"

"I'm really sick of Indian."

"Esther? Me too."

"Why do we keep going?" I asked him.

"I thought you liked it."

"I thought *you* liked it," I said.

He shook his head, smiling. I was leaving in eight days. If I was going to talk to him and Mom about the idea I'd had, I was going to have to do it soon.

7 DAYS LEFT

I started to wonder: What did it actually meant to *not be a wimp*? Maybe, kind of like when I'd talked to Mom over Thanksgiving, it meant asking someone to describe their butterfly. How else were you supposed to compare it to your hands?

On Saturday afternoon, Dad and I sat at the tiny kitchen table. He poured me some coffee (he'd insisted on decaf, since it was afternoon) and handed me the hazelnut creamer.

"Dad?" I said, taking a sip. "I have an idea and I don't want you to say yes or no until I explain everything, 'kay?"

He looked confused. "Okay."

I pulled out my phone to FaceTime Mom. When her face appeared (a dab of white paint on her cheek), I began to talk. "I want to propose something," I told the two of them. "I don't want to leave North Carolina. I want to stay here second semester."

Neither of them said anything.

"That's it," I told them. "That's my proposal. I mean, it doesn't have anything to do with either of you. It's just that I have these new friends here and I don't want to leave them yet."

Finally, Dad cleared his throat. "What do you think?" he asked Mom.

"Dad and I will talk," Mom told me.

6 DAYS LEFT

It was suddenly warm again.

"My mom and I have been texting a lot," I told Ollie. We were lying in Annabella and Damien's hammock.

"Yeah? That's awesome! Tell me more."

"I don't know. It feels different. In a good way. More like it used to back when I was in elementary school. It's weird that she and I saw things so differently." I put my thumbs together. "Butterfly . . ."

Ollie squeezed them. Their hands were so warm. "Hands."

5 DAYS LEFT

Ollie and I were in their yard, watching Froggy sleep in a new hutch Ollie had made for her.

"Es?" Ollie asked nervously.

"Yeah?"

"What made you stop liking me? You know, after the spinny-spin."

"What?" I asked, stunned. "I *never* stopped liking you."

"I was worried that you weren't attracted to me because I'm nonbinary."

I could barely speak. "That was never it. Maybe I panicked?" I admitted, thinking of how I'd felt ditched by Mom. And how before she and Dad had told me about the divorce, at least I'd been able to hope that they would become more like Emily's parents.

Now there was officially no hope.

"You know, it's okay," Ollie told me, reading my mind. "It's okay to be sad."

3 DAYS LEFT

For days, Mom and Dad had been looking into whether or not they could get a refund from my school in Saint Louis and whether or not, even if they could, it was a good idea for me to stay. The decision would be a last-minute one. *Don't get your hopes up*, they continually reminded me.

Weeks before, Dad had bought a gallon of white paint, some brushes, and a drop cloth. They'd been sitting in the corner of my room, waiting. He didn't want us rushing to paint at the last minute, so now Ollie and I stood together, paintbrushes in hand. Time was flying by. I most likely only had three days left.

2 DAYS LEFT

It was a cool, clear night. We were side by side, under the stars.

I turned to Ollie. "A while ago, I got an idea," I told them. They looked kind of nervous.

"I asked my parents if I could stay with my dad for the rest of the year. *Here*. Because it didn't seem fair for them to uproot me twice in seventh grade, and why should I have to go home now? I don't *want* to go home now."

Ollie sat up eagerly. "And?" they asked quickly.

1 DAY LEFT

The hammock swung gently. Our force fields combined, doubling the electricity, and it was exactly like that night back in September, except that everything was different.

We turned to each other—just-Ollie and just-Essie. Smiled. I wondered: What would be left if all I had was this feeling, right now? What would exist for me if all the words were gone?

Nothing?

Our lips touched.

Or everything?

Zap.

PART 2

HANDS

DAY 1

Everything—*everything* changed when I saw her.

I'd been walking to my locker, psyching myself up with a *you're going to kill it with your mad combination-lock-opening skills* pep talk when I'd glanced to my left . . . and spotted her. *The new girl.* Whoever had been behind me bumped into my back and my inner Ollie rolled their eyes at me. But I couldn't move; I was powerless in her presence.

She was looking nervously from her schedule to the locker numbers, and it dawned on me: She's probably Esther Rosenberg, the girl Mom had told me to introduce myself to.

But I didn't. I couldn't. All I could do was visualize this show Dad and I had watched on the science channel the night before. Lightning storms in space. Storm chasers in the ionosphere. I felt the blood pumping in and out of my heart in electromagnetic pulses, exploding like space lightning in bursts of blue and red.

DAY 2

"Spill it," Lucy said, waving her hand in front of my face to get my attention.

"What?" I asked, turning to her and Savannah. They both burst out laughing.

Savannah packed her empty Tupperware into her lunch bag and turned around to see what I'd been staring at (*who* I'd been staring at) throughout lunch. "The new girl?" she asked, smiling.

Lucy looked over her shoulder. "Wait, you let her eat *all by herself*?" she asked. Esther was getting up from the back table to throw out her garbage.

"I didn't . . . I mean, I couldn't—"

"She's nice," Savannah interrupted, saving me from trying to explain this *thing* that I had no words for. "I met her in class yesterday. I'll ask her to eat with us tomorrow, you wimp," she joked. "Her name's Essie."

Essie.

DAY 3

"Hey, did you have a chance to introduce yourself to Esther?" Mom asked after school, poking her head into the living room, spatula in hand, as I fed a handful of pellets to Froggy who (a) still elicited bad memories, and (b) *definitely* wasn't a dog.

"She goes by *Essie*, Mom," I told her, more emphatically than I'd meant to.

"I'll take that as a yes," she said, looking at me curiously, before disappearing back into the kitchen to flip the fried tofu. (Really, Mom? Tofu again?)

I thought back to art and science. And to lunch. I'd watched from the doorway as Savannah had called Essie over, and she and Lucy had proceeded to introduce her to the world. They'd told her the name of each person sitting at our lunch table as I'd stared, starstruck.

"And that's Ollie," Lucy had finally said, smiling at me, once I'd built up the courage to join them. I'd felt a tightening pressure in my chest, like a hand clasping a doorknob.

DAY 5

Ollie: Hi

Savannah: Hi!

Luciana: Hey O

Ollie: Heyo so I have a deep question for you guys. So u know how I'm like the poster child for the happy nonbinary middle schooler?

Savannah: 100%

Luciana: 1000% . . . why?

Ollie: Do you think when someone new sees me they see a happy nonbinary middle schooler or do they like see MORE

Savannah: That's deep

Luciana: My brain hurts.
By someone new u don't
happen to mean essie
do you?

Ollie: Maybe? I mean yes
obviously

Savannah: Lol I don't
know?

Luciana: I honestly don't
know either

Ollie: Right?

DAY 6

"What's the word on GLOW?" Mom asked, sitting down on the couch with me, pretending (failing) to be chill, which was how she always acted when talking about GLOW. I wondered why it hadn't bothered me before.

"What do you mean?" I asked, looking from my algebra notes to my computer. Why did math have to exist?

"Is everything good to go?"

I closed my notebook and examined the creases on Mom's forehead. They softened when I smiled at her. "Yup, good to go. Ms. Rose just sent me a link to the calendar. The weekly lunch meetings, after-school meetings, and my individual meetings with Ms. Rose are all set up through June."

"Great!" Mom replied quickly. "Do you want to brainstorm any projects or initiatives together?"

I fought the urge to roll my eyes. I'd never minded Mom's help before. But now "Initiative Number One" was: *How to get Essie to join GLOW so I have an excuse to talk to her.* "Nah, that's okay," I told Mom. "I've got this."

DAY 8

Ollie

Max

Hey maxi pad

Hey Ol Doll

I have a crush on mom's new colleague's daughter.

Nice! That's awesome ☺ Don't overwhelm her with too much Ollie!

Thx for the vote of confidence

Don't tell mom she'll just meddle

More than usual? I thought u didn't mind mom's meddling

I didn't used to

Your secret is safe. Keep
me posted!

DAY 10

"Bad news, Ollie." Mr. Lee approached me at my locker (where I was *slaying* it with my combination lock. Sixth day in a row!). "I had to swap your math and P.E. classes. Scheduling snafu."

I popped open my lock as he handed me a new schedule.

"You're not upset with the change," he noted, observing my smile.

"Nope," I told him. "All good." Because now I had gym with Lucy and Savannah. *And Essie.* I gathered my notebooks happily. Then all the synapses finally connected in my brain and I realized that gym with Lucy, Savannah, and Essie meant changing in the locker room *with Essie.*

Which might mean Essie thinking I was a girl.

And also? Changing in a locker room with your crush? *Awkward.*

DAY 15

"Hey! Want a job?" I asked Essie when she showed up at her locker, where I was waiting for her after school.

"Hello to you, too," she replied, tucking her hair behind her ears. God, she was adorable.

"Please?" I fake begged (okay, *actually* begged). "We have approximately one billion posters to hang up." I pulled the photocopied GLOW flyers out of my backpack and handed the stack to her.

She flipped through them. Looked back at me. I thought about how she'd misinterpreted my comment about Panda and Penelope last week. How she's been overly eager to tell me she was cool with my gender. And how she seemed to *get* that I wouldn't have been hanging out with her if I didn't think she was. "What are they for?" she asked.

"GLOW Club. Gender and Love Open-minded Warriors. We're going to erase all the hate in the world."

She nodded, not looking away. "I hate hate."

The tugging feeling returned to my chest, like Essie's hand tightening around the doorknob.

DAY 16

Lucy   **Ollie**

Waz up

                              Hi Lucifer

I just want to tell u that this
yr Savvy and I joined GLOW
just to watch u and essie flirt

                              Do u think she likes me

I think she loves u

And u know what I'd do to her
if ur gender became an
ISSUE lol

                              Ur so scary

IKR?

DAY 17

"Hey, mini me!" Annabella called out from my front porch, where they were drinking tea with Mom after school on Wednesday. I cut across the lawn and joined the two of them.

"Hey, hon!" Mom ruffled my hair as I reached for the plate of cookies.

"You guys having a tea party?" I joked.

"Nah, just gossiping," Mom said.

"Anything good?"

"Well, the Acostas seem to be getting quotes on a new roof," Mom told me.

"And Marta from around the corner neglected to pick up her dog's poop. *Again*," Annabella added.

I laughed, thinking of all the hours I'd spent on the porch over the past several years talking to Annabella. Unlike their conversations with Mom, we didn't talk about our neighbors and dog poop. Instead, we mostly chatted about how it feels to be nonbinary—the challenges, the general awesomeness. Our *gender journeys*, as Annabella liked to call them, had been similar, except for two major differences, which were that when Annabella had been a kid, they hadn't fully understood their gender, and they'd had to keep their identity a secret. Over the years, they'd told me a lot about a summer camp for queer kids where they'd worked, and how helping kids be themselves had also helped them.

"You guys are so weird," I told Mom and Annabella, knowing they'd both take it as a compliment, as I grabbed another cookie off the plate.

"Thank you," they replied in unison.

DAY 20

I lay in bed, feeling like the world's biggest idiot, as I stared at the glow-in-the-dark solar system on my ceiling that Max had given me right before he left for college. Just when things had started to feel like . . . *something* with Essie, I'd ruined it.

I turned over, trying to get comfortable. The question she'd asked me earlier that day about GLOW membership was *totally* normal: *When do we stop trying to get new members and move on to other stuff?*

I could have so easily said, *We'll move on to other stuff soon, but we'll never stop trying to get new members.*

Instead, I'd acted weird. I didn't want to have to explain to her that even though I loved being an advocate, I hated that I had to explain my existence; even though I loved being the poster child for the Happy Nonbinary Kid, I was a happy nonbinary kid plus a million other things. When I was with Essie, I just wanted to *be*. I wanted her to like me. Like, *like me* like me. The way I liked her. And it felt like maybe she did. Or she *had*.

Until this afternoon.

DAY 21

Ollie **Lucy**

Lucy, help

> Waz up

I think I ruined something

> Okay

Stop being so calm HELP

> OKAY! What did u do?

I ruined things with Essie

> Doubtful she totes loves u

I kinda acted weird when she asked me abt GLOW membership

And ur mission to recruit
the world?

Lol yes

Talk to her about it?

Blah. K.

DAY 22

"So we've never actually talked about it—the gender stuff. You know. How I am. What it's like." My heart was thudding, leaking beats of red and blue electricity, as we sat on my living room floor.

Essie tilted her head to the side, waiting for me to go on. Fazed but unfazed. Perfect.

"It's just that I sort of have to be an advocate sometimes. Like, raise awareness and educate people, which can be exhausting and annoying. But at the same time, I kind of love it. It's weird."

"I get that." She scratched Froggy's nose, never taking her eyes off mine.

"And I have to bring people together, so nobody feels *alone*," I continued, handing Froggy over to her. She took him gently. "I mean, people need to know that lots of people like me exist. I'm not *that* unique."

"Okay," she replied. "You just always seem so comfortable with yourself. I didn't think the gender thing was an issue for you."

I got the sense that Essie saw me as way more together than I felt. I took off the Sox cap that Max had sent me from Chicago and ran my fingers through my hair. "It's not," I told her truthfully.

"I'm confused," she said, smiling a little, like she didn't *really* mind being confused.

"Can we be confused together?" I asked her.

"Forever."

"Or," I said, "at least until you ditch me in December."

DAY 23

I waited for Essie on the corner. It was the first cool night of the year and I tucked my hands into my sweatshirt pockets. I kind of couldn't believe that Mom and Dad had agreed to let me out this late at night to show Essie the moon.

"Come on, Marianne, it does look really cool tonight," Dad had said to Mom, winking at me like he had my back.

Up ahead, a thin figure in flip-flops and sweatpants, black against the deep-gray sky, turned the corner, waved, and sped up.

"You got out of prison!" I joked when she crossed the street. She smelled like shampoo. Behind us, the moon was a tangerine slice in the crook of a tree branch. It brightened the tree, the street, her. "Turn around," I told her.

She did, taking a tiny step closer to me because she *wanted* to be near me. The ache in my chest returned.

"Whoa," Essie said, looking up. "That's incredible!"

DAY 24

Ollie

Max

MAX I'M IN LOVE

Who is this

SHUT UP!!

Srsly that's awesome tell
me everything

I want her to understand
everything abt my gender.
I like talking to her abt it!

I can just be me with her. I
mean me plus the advocate
stuff. It's like she thinks I'm
really cool and confident

Aren't you?

Um, NO?

Whatever it's confusing

I really like her DON'T TELL
MOM AND DAD they'll just be
annoying

MAX

Promise! Does she like
you too?!?!

I think so?!

♥

DAY 25

I stood in front of my mirror, ran some gel through the long part of my hair, and adjusted my unbuttoned flannel over my tank top. Turning to the side to assess my level of awesomeness, I said my daily silent prayer to the God of Chest Size that mine wouldn't get *too* much bigger, because this sports bra I was wearing, with its cool Nike swoosh on the front? I could totally handle it. No problem. A *bra* bra? That would be a different story.

Then I went to the front porch. To wait for Essie.

When she arrived, we ducked through the bushes to Annabella and Damien's yard, where we lay back in their hammock. The gentle swinging should have been calming, but instead, my heart thumped, reminding me of Froggy when she used to freak out in her cage when we first got her. *Calm down, Ollie*, I told myself forcefully. *Remember your four, seven, eight breathing from health class*. I inhaled for four counts. Held my breath for seven. Exhaled for eight. Turned to Essie. "Hey," I whispered. The moon was a pale crescent. It made her eyes shine.

She turned to me, the shine disappearing into shadows. "Hey." I looked at her lips, gray in the night. So close to mine. I felt like Essie could see all of me—even the parts I couldn't see. And she liked *everything*. It was perfect. Except I didn't know what to do next. So I looked back at the moon. She did the same, leaning her head against mine.

DAY 27

It was 10:45 on Saturday night. I couldn't sleep. When the light faded completely from my glow-in-the-dark stickers, I got up the nerve to text Essie. *You up?*

I practiced my deep breathing and thought about the electromagnetic pulse. The red and blue electricity. The doorway that Essie was pulling open.

What was the deal with the doorway, anyway? I mean, what was behind it? As Essie cracked it open, energy leaked out of me like I was a radio and the energy was radio waves, or like I was a fire and the energy was heat. It made the air around me hum and waver and glow, just like when you turn on a lightsaber.

My phone buzzed. It was Essie. *You still there?*

Yup, I replied. I'm here.

DAY 28

The spinny-spin whirled through the darkening night. It was humid; the air hung in a mist around us and the electric waves bursting from my body bounced off minuscule water particles in the haze, creating something amazing—invisible but amazing. And *obvious*.

Until ... it wasn't.

The electric glow flickered, like something broke the spell. Or, like *someone* broke it.

I turned to Essie and the droplets of light fell. I imagined my glow-in-the-dark stars plunging to Earth. I couldn't read Essie's face, but she had pulled the doorway wide open and words—labels for ideas and feelings that I hadn't thought of since before I'd come out as nonbinary, back in fourth grade—covered me. I wanted these words; I needed them. But something didn't feel right. That *something* was coming from Essie.

The words buried me, just as my lips touched hers.

DAY 29

When Mom came in to tell me to hurry up or I'd be late for school, I was still in bed, my pillow over my head. "I can't go," I told her.

"Why not?" she asked quickly, trying (failing) to sound calm. "Did something happen with Essie last night?"

I thought of the kiss—of how it seemed like it was going to be perfect, until something had shifted in Essie. And how that something *had* to be the fact that I'm nonbinary. I mean, I knew that Essie didn't *generally* dislike me because of my gender. But it had to be the reason why she didn't *like me* like me.

I didn't answer Mom, and in the moment of silence, I could practically hear the gears rotating in her brain: *Aha! I knew something was going on between them and Essie! OMG, something went wrong . . . It's probably gender-related. THEIR SELF-ESTEEM!*

"Do you want to take a mental health day?" she asked fake calmly.

I moved the pillow. "Can I?"

She smiled, sat down, ruffled my hair. "Sure. Want to talk about anything?"

"No," I said, probably too quickly. "Thanks, but no."

Later that morning, Mom sent me over to Annabella and Damien's with banana bread.

"Perfect timing," Annabella said when they answered the door. "I just got off a work call, and Damien isn't teaching today. Dame! Ollie's here!" they called down to the basement. I noticed that Annabella didn't ask why I wasn't at school, proving that Mom had definitely told them *something* was up.

"Annabella," I asked them when we sat down at their kitchen table, "do you ever feel overwhelmed by all the things in your head?"

Damien poured us hot water for tea. Fancy.

"Always," they said. "Careful, it's burning."

"So . . . I can see the steam. I *am* thirteen," I reminded them (not) jokingly.

"Seriously," Damien chimed in, rolling his eyes at Annabella. "Ollie, you should try woodworking. Best therapy ever. Want me to show you a thing or two?"

"Really?" I had told Ms. Rose I'd finish the video we'd been editing to advertise GLOW on the school website, but . . . the thought of making something—with my own two hands—seemed like just what I needed. "Sure!" I told him.

DAY 30

When I'd gotten home from Intro to Woodworking with Damien, Mom looked calmer. Or, at least, more like her typical self. "Hey!" she'd said, catching me before I could disappear into my room.

"Hey." I'd been picking a splinter out of my thumb.

"I just got off a call. So the Sociology Department has been thinking for a while that they'd like to sponsor an event at your school. We were able to get a permit for December fourth to march on campus. You know, like a pride event. Any interest in doing the planning and heading it up with GLOW?"

For a second, I'd felt . . . *something*. It was like Mom was reminding me of my role as the Happy Nonbinary Kid. But then I'd reminded myself how lucky I was to have an over-the-top supportive family. And of how much I *liked* being a happy nonbinary kid. I mean, it's who I was. Except for when Essie wasn't enjoying our kiss because she wasn't attracted to me.

It was confusing. Also, I hadn't seen Mom in full-on protective-mother mode since fourth grade, when I'd come out as nonbinary. GLOW had grown into something awesome since Mom had given me the idea to start it as a way to channel the elementary school crap into productivity. So, even though I didn't mean it *completely*, I'd said, "Thanks, Mom."

Then I'd gone to my room, texted the whole story of the terrible kiss to Lucy and Savannah, and waited for three o'clock when their afternoon classes would be over and they'd be allowed to turn their phones on again.

At lunch on Tuesday, I made the announcement to the members of GLOW: "What do you think about an event sponsored by the Sociology Department, on campus, the week after Thanksgiving? A Thankful for Pride event!" I watched Essie as I spoke. Her eyes followed me, just like they always had. She *seemed* to still like me; *like me* like me, even. But obviously, based on the kiss, I was reading her wrong.

DAY 32

Max   **Ollie**

U up, Ol Doll

It's 6:46 am, Maxi Pad

Did I wake you?

What did Mom tell you

"Check in"

Don't you have, like,
college to attend?

Perhaps

I'm fine

What's going on

I dunno it's confusing

Want to talk about it

No I've got this

U sure

I'll let u know if I need help

Promise

Promise

DAY 33

"Did you ask her to come to the planning meeting?" Savannah prodded as I shoved my sweatshirt into my locker before social studies.

"You're such a bully," I joked, running my hands over my newly cut hair. I loved the extra-soft spiky feel. "I asked her."

Savannah gave me a thumbs-up. "And she's coming?"

"She's coming."

"Are we actually going to plan for the march, or are Luciana and I just going to watch you guys stare at each other?"

I laughed, even though it wasn't *exactly* funny, because I didn't understand what was going on between Essie and me. "I guess we'll find out soon." I wiggled my eyebrows at Savannah.

After school, Lucy, Savannah, Essie, and I walked to my house. I tried really, really hard to calm my hyper-Ollie brain as we fed Froggy some alfalfa and opened a box of cookies, but I could feel my mind starting to wander: I mean, what had gone wrong when we had kissed? And, somewhat related, was it possible that people were surrounded by invisible, magnetic dust and maybe, every once in a while, a person with a certain, special type of positively charged dust might come across another person with a certain, special type of negatively charged dust, causing their entire beings to pull together and—

"Does that sound good to you, Ol?" Savannah asked, wiping a cookie crumb from her lip.

"Um . . ."

"To start a to-do list," Lucy added, helping me out, trying not to smile.

"Great idea," I said, grabbing a notebook from my backpack and writing *Thankful for Pride Event* across the top. When I looked back up at Essie, her head was bent slightly to the side, like she was trying to figure me out.

DAY 34

"How'd you get into woodworking?" I asked Damien once we'd attached hinges to the box that he and I had started making the previous Monday. I'd spent the entire morning in his workshop carving a design onto its cover with the pyrography pen. A fire-writing pen! How amazing was that?

"I needed a hobby. Teaching at the university is stressful. There's something about making something—"

"With your own hands?" I interrupted.

"Totally."

"It gets you out of your head," I continued.

He laughed. "Maybe you're actually *my* mini me!" I liked that idea. I mean, I liked the idea of being his *and* Annabella's mini me.

We called Annabella downstairs to check out the finished box. "Wow!" they said.

"Thanks!"

"I meant 'Wow, you still have ten fingers,'" they joked. "Seriously though? It's great!"

"Yeah, *and* I'm usually a terrible artist!"

"Woodworking uses a whole different set of brain muscles," Damien explained. "So what are we—I mean *you*—going to make next?"

"I have no clue."

"I guess we'll just have to wait for the muse to bring you an idea."

DAY 36

Dad **Ollie**

Hey, kiddo

> Hey dad waz up

Not much, you?

> How's life at the law firm
> this afternoon

Amazing as always ☺

> What time will u be
> home

6:30ish barring any drama
How are you doing today?

> Tell Mom I said I'm great!

Man you're smart

> Also tell Mom I'm not a

baby. And I love her. And she's awesome. And I love u, too.

Any other messages? ☺

I'm 13

I'm 49 and I don't have all the answers.

K

I'm just saying we're here if you need us.

I no

Know

I know

DAY 38

After school, I brought Froggy out to the back porch, pulled the baby gate across the top of the steps so she wouldn't escape, and set her down on a chair. Then I pulled two apples out of my hoodie pockets—one for her, one for me. My phone rang as I took a bite.

"Hey, O!" Lucy said as I answered her FaceTime call. She was in the school gym.

I propped the phone on an empty chair so she could watch Froggy nibble her apple. "When's your game?" I asked.

"Not for five minutes," Savannah said, her face joining Lucy's on the screen. "Hi, Frog! That's plenty of time for you to spill it, Ol. What's going on with Essie?"

I shrugged, chewing, thinking about the fact that Lucy and Savannah and I pretty much only talked about Essie these days. "No idea."

"She totally still likes you," Lucy told me.

"Loves you," Savannah chimed in.

"Loves you," Lucy agreed.

"Weird, right?" I asked as Lucy looked behind her at the stands. "Who are you looking for?"

"Nobody," she answered, grinning, as Savannah grabbed the phone.

"*Peter*," Savannah whispered, laughing.

"Peter?" I asked, picking up the phone. Lucy liked Peter Mason? When did *that* happen?

"Shush," Lucy insisted to me.

"You think if Peter is in the stands, he's going to hear me on your phone?" I teased, while suddenly feeling like an outsider to Lucy's life. "Hey, when did you start liking him?"

"We have to go. Coach is calling us over," Savannah said. "Later, O!"

"Later," I said, hanging up the phone. *And why did Savannah know about this crush before me?*

DAY 40

Ollie

Lucy

Hey Lucifer

Heyo

Spill it about peter!
Why didn't you tell me?

No reason! It's kinda
new. He's nice and smart
and cute!

I agree with all those things!
Have u talked to him?

About anything besides
chess club? Um no

Oh ☹ is it a secret? Who
knows?

Just u and Savvy. You
can tell Essie. I don't
care if she knows. Gotta
go my mom is yelling at
us to clean basement!

Byeeee!

Ollie

Essie

Hey Es!

Hi!

Whatcha doing?

HW. Boring. You?

Avoiding HW. So have you
ever felt weird because your
BFF tells things to other
people and you should know
about it first but you've been
like left out

Are you reading my
mind? 1000%

Right now something like
that is happening with
Emily my bff at home.

Like literally this exact
second

Seriously?

Yes! You too?

Yeah Lucy told Savvy
that she has a crush on
peter before she told me.

I don't wanna be petty. It's
not a big deal but it feels
like a big deal

Um Ollie?

Yeah?

Did you seriously not
know Lucy has a crush
on Peter? No offense
but all you needed were
eyes to know that

Are you serious?! You
knew?

I could tell!

I feel like an idiot

You're not an idiot

You're nice

IKR ♥

DAY 42

I looked at the bulletin board on my wall—at the picture of me and Lucy, back in fourth grade, each holding up a giant slice of pizza. At the blue Field Day ribbon I'd won for the 100-meter dash in fifth grade. The Worst First Kiss Ever was like a doorway that Essie had pulled open, revealing a path that led backward, to elementary school. Instead of doing my algebra homework or revising the GLOW mission statement that Ms. Rose had helped me write, I opened my laptop and googled Rumble Peak Amusement Park. I scrolled through some images, but looking at the rides and attractions made me feel anxious and nauseous. I closed the computer.

"Do you think it's strange that I'm a girl who likes boy things?" I remember asking Dad back in third grade. It must not have been long after Mom had taken me for my first *big* haircut, because that was when I'd started to get questions from people at school (which was annoying) and misgendered as a boy in public (which was awesome). Dad and I had been tossing a baseball in the yard.

"There's no such thing as—" I remember him starting, but I'd cut him off.

"Yeah, yeah, there's no such thing as 'boys' things' and 'girls' things.'"

"Did someone say something to you?" he had asked.

"People always say things to me. About having short hair, and wearing boys'"—I'd cut myself off—"clothes from the quote unquote boys' department," I'd corrected, tossing him the ball.

"Nice throw!" Then he'd asked, "Do *you* think it's weird?"

I'd caught his pop fly. "Yeah, maybe, but in a good way. I'm *good* weird."

He'd laughed, catching my grounder. "Good weird, huh?" he'd asked. "That's a *good* term."

I opened the computer now to my math assignment, but I couldn't focus, so I wandered into the kitchen, where Mom was checking her email.

Dad was at the stove stirring some weird-smelling soup. "Dad? Do we still have our baseball gloves?" I asked him.

He looked up from the pot. "I'd imagine so," he said. "Maybe in the shed?" Our shed was home to all the world's

grossest animals: mice, raccoons, spiders . . . so many spiders . . . "You want to toss the ball around?" he asked.

"Maybe some other time. I was just wondering."

"Hey, Adam," Mom interrupted, "when's dinner going to
be ready? I want to hop on a quick call with Walter."

Dad and I exchanged a glance. Mom "hopping on a call"
with Essie's dad usually translated to Mom counseling
Walter on his marriage issues. "Half an hour?"

"Are you going to go all couple's-counselor on him, Mom?"
I asked.

She wiggled her eyebrows at me. Maybe she had finally
realized that I'd outgrown spilling *everything* about *everything* and accepted the fact that she'd have to get her "ther-
apist fix" elsewhere. All good. Walter obviously needed a
friend.

DAY 45

I dropped my backpack on the kitchen floor and leaned over Mom's shoulder. "Hey, Maxi Pad!" I said, waving at the phone, which was propped up against her half-empty coffee cup.

"What's up, Ol?" Max asked from his dorm room in Chicago. "Mom was just telling me all about your idea for the rally in December. Sounds awesome!"

"Yeah, that was actually Mom's idea, but thanks."

"Ah. Anyway, so I was telling Mom that Joey still works at Campus Press. I just texted him and asked him to help you publicize. He texted back immediately and said yes. Obviously."

Don't be annoyed, Ollie. You're so lucky; your family is seriously fantastic. Mom was beaming. Man, I loved her for this. For everything. Max, too.

"Great, tell him thanks," I said. And I meant it. But I also felt like changing the subject. "What's new with you?"

"Not much. It's pretty here now. Look." He pointed his phone out the window. Red and orange trees dotted the campus below him.

"Nice!"

"How are classes going?" Mom asked, which was my cue to leave, since things were about to get boring, so I poked my head in front of hers.

"I'm out. Bye, Maxi."

"Later, Ol."

"And tell Joey thanks," I repeated, despite the nagging knowledge that I could *definitely* handle things myself.

DAY 47

I looked around the lunch table that Friday at our weekly GLOW meeting. Including me, we had fourteen members. Mom had gotten a text from Max the night before and had knocked on my bedroom door to tell me the good news just as Joey had messaged me: *Great news, O!*

It turned out that, thanks to a connection Joey had, in addition to Campus Press covering the pride event, ABC News would be there. "You'll definitely increase membership once you announce this school-wide," Mom had told me. "People will want to be on the news."

"But do we want members who are participating just because they want to be on TV?" I'd wondered aloud.

"Ol, it doesn't matter how you get them on board, as long as they're on board."

I felt like, with all this involvement from Mom and Max and Joey, and now ABC News, I was playing a smaller and smaller role in this project. But maybe Mom was right. And the more publicity the better.

So I tried to channel her energy as I made my announcement. "I have excellent news!" I said, looking out over the other thirteen members, trying not to stare at Essie. Lucy gave me an encouraging nod. "My brother's best friend from high school is Joey Chen, and he works for Campus Press, which is covering the Thankful for Pride march. Joey wanted to help us out, so he submitted our info to ABC News. Now ABC wants to do a thing on us, too!"

Everyone cheered. Essie smiled at me, her eyes locked on mine, like she *believed* in me. Like she had no doubt that I could do anything in the world. And maybe I could. But with all this help from all these amazing people in my life, how would I ever know?

DAY 51

After school, Lucy, Savannah, Essie, and I met at my locker, where I took out the massive stack of brightly colored flyers that Dad had photocopied for me at his office the night before and the packages of blue sticky tack that Ms. Rose had *absolutely insisted* we use to hang them. For the next hour, we plastered the hallways, doorways, and lockers with information about the Thankful for Pride march *and* ABC News coverage. Then, exhausted and starving, we began to make our way back toward the seventh-grade hall, only to realize that *blue sticky tack doesn't stick.*

"No!" Lucy said, picking up a poster, smudges of sticky tack on each of its four corners. "Just, no," she said again, pretending to cry as she looked up and down the hallway at all the fallen and dangling posters.

Savannah lay down on the floor and closed her eyes. "I

can't," she announced. "Wake me up when you're done rehanging them. Or if anyone finds a pizza."

"I'm new here. I can still get away with *anything*," Essie joked. Then she disappeared into a classroom and emerged with four rolls of masking tape. "If anyone asks about the tape, blame it on me."

I smiled at her boldness. At *her*.

For the next hour, we rehung the flyers. Essie and I worked together: She rolled tape loops, and I stuck them onto the papers. It felt like she wanted to be with me. Like, right next to me. "You know how amazing all of this is, how amazing *you* are," she told me, "right?"

DAY 53

Thursday's GLOW meeting was *packed*.

I reminded myself of Mom's words: "It doesn't matter how you get them on board, as long as they're on board." The benches around the lunch table were crowded with sixth, seventh, and eighth graders talking, laughing, eating their lunches, and waiting for me to start the meeting.

Essie got up on her knees so she could see everyone and counted the number of people. She caught my eye, held up three fingers on each hand, and mouthed, *Thirty-three!* Then she gave me two thumbs-up. Lucy, who was sitting behind her, looked from the back of her head to me and gave me two thumbs-up, too.

Nineteen new GLOW members. All because of Max's connection to Joey and Joey's connection to ABC.

And before that, because of Mom's idea for the rally.

It had been Mom's idea, too, for me to start GLOW when

I'd entered sixth grade. Which made me think of fifth grade. And fourth grade. Rumble Peak. Addison Miller.

I tried to clear my head. *So you've got amazing support from family and friends. Deal with it, Ollie,* I told myself. And I went to work, calling the meeting to order, describing the December 4 rally, assigning jobs. And Essie—the way she looked at me throughout it all—she was *impressed*. I could feel it.

Intensely.

DAY 54

 Essie

 Ollie

Hey O!

Hey Es!

Is everything ok with you and Luc

Yes! Does it not seem ok?

It seems fine! Just wondering cause of our last textversation

Oh yeah. No it's good. I really want peter to like her!

Maybe he does! Maybe

she should talk to him
about it

That would take LOTS of
guts

So many guts. All the glow
stuff is really cool. I'm
impressed with u

U are?!

Yeah you do all these
awesome things

Only glow actually

That's a lot!

Is it?

You say that like there's
something else you'd
wanna do

Really? Dunno. I'm
always so busy erasing
hate lol

U could do other things
too if u wanted!

You think?

Um, obviously? I'm sure u
could make time

My moms yelling at me
to clean the bunny's
cage

The duck's cage?

Yeah!

Bye!

DAY 57

After lunch, Essie and I walked together toward our lockers. The night before, when we'd met at the library, the feeling of electricity between us had been so strong that I could have picked up a mound of magnetized air and *actually* held it in my hands.

At the same time, when we'd been making plans, she'd shot me down when I'd asked her about doing homework at her house. (Come to think of it, she pretty much shot me down *every* time the idea of going to her house came up.)

Up ahead, a crowd had gathered around the Activities Board. The next session of clubs had been posted. "Let's look," Essie said, dragging me over. We inched our way toward the sign-up sheets.

"Do you want to join something?" I asked her.

"Not really," she said. "I'm just curious."

Back in fourth grade, I'd developed an aversion to activities, in general. *Girls' soccer. Boys' baseball. Daddy-daughter sport night.* Everything about these gendered teams and clubs was so . . . dumb. Once I'd realized that my label was "nonbinary," Mom, Dad, Max, and Annabella started to pound the idea into my head until I'd understood that the world—*the binary*—was wrong. *I* was awesome just the way I was.

I read through the sheets anyway; at Lab it was just the sports that were gendered. *Cool Coders.* Snooze. *Chess Masters.* Oh my God, boring, though I'd never say so to Lucy, who could *run* that club. Wait—*Stage Combat?* That was new. I pointed it out to Essie and read the description to myself. *Learn the art of stage fighting and stage weaponry with Ms. Wigg, complete with stage makeup and costumes, and a performance in the spring!* "Whoa," I told Essie. "That sounds amazing."

"Why can I *totally* see you doing that? Sign up!"

"I don't think I have time," I told her, thinking of my twice-a-week, after-school GLOW meetings, the weekly lunch meetings, *and* planning for the march.

"Ollie," she said, turning to me, her long hair falling over my arm, "you're like Superma—Superperson. If you want to do it, I'm *sure* you can make time."

I laughed. "You think?" I asked.

"I do."

So I put my name on the list.

DAY 58

"Okay," I said to Damien when he opened the door for me after dinner. "I have an idea. I know what my next project is going to be."

"Hello to you, too."

"So my art teacher showed us these optical illusions and they're awesome. I want to carve something that can look like two hands, with the thumbs pressed together *or* like a butterfly." I held up my hands to show him.

"Cool!" he said, leaning against the doorframe, thinking.

"Yeah, so can I come in or what?"

"Sorry, just trying to decide how we—I mean *you*—should approach that." He stepped to the side and ushered me into the kitchen. "Come to the basement. If Annabella gets home and the dirty dishes are still in the sink, I'm blaming it on you."

"Deal."

Downstairs, Damien told me all about the different kinds of woods, and how butternut was a good beginner's wood when it came to carving. He pulled out the carving gloves and made me promise to always wear them because he liked all ten of my fingers. Then he lined up the gouges and chisels and gave me a lesson on each. Finally, before heading back up to do the dishes, he allowed me to get my (gloved) hands on a hunk of wood.

Carving was cool because, in a way, it was the opposite of drawing. It was creating something by taking away, not adding to. By the time Dad came by to tell me to come home (homework and *another* revision on the GLOW mission statement awaited), I'd made a decent dent in one side of the wooden block.

I thanked Damien as we left. "That was awesome," I told him. "Can I come back tomorrow?"

"My house is your house, Ollie," he told me. "See you then."

DAY 59

At the first Stage Combat meeting, after a PowerPoint introducing us to the rules and fake weapons and fake bodily
fluids that we could produce using the fake weapons, Ms.
Wigg pulled out the props and helped me wrap a "blood-
soaked" bandage around my hand. I held it up, admiring it.
Man, this was amazing.

Then I hopped onto the stage with the rest of the crew.
"My name is Zoey," a hyper-in-a-good-way sixth grader
yelled, approaching me, wooden sword in hand. "You killed
my father. Prepare to die."

"*The Princess Bride*! Sweet!" I said as she plunged her sword
into my stomach and I fell. "I love that movie!"

"Me too!" She helped me up just in time for me to punch
her in the cheek, sending her rolling backward.

"Remember, it's all about tricking the audience!" Ms. Wigg

yelled as Zoey got up and clocked me in the face. I chomped down on a blood capsule and died, sweet red liquid dripping down my chin.

As I lay on the stage, I thought of how Max had responded when I'd first texted him about Essie. *Don't overwhelm her with too much Ollie!* he'd warned. Stage combat was all about being *too much*. I hopped up, grabbed a rapier, and wiped the blood off my face with the back of my hand. "En garde!" I yelled. Zoey tried (and failed) to keep a straight face as I stabbed her in the gut.

After activities, Lucy came over to my house. We sat at the kitchen table eating raisins dipped in peanut butter and (not) doing homework. "So everyone doing stage combat seems cool?" she asked nonchalantly after telling me what was going on with Peter (which was that he had said hi to her when she had walked into Chess Club).

"They're the coolest people in the school," I joked.

"You know what I mean."

I did. She meant *gender*-cool. As in, is anyone messing with you? And I loved her for it, even though she was reminding me of Mom.

"Everyone's cool," I confirmed, though. "I don't think there are any more Addison Millers in my future."

Lucy looked startled. I hadn't brought up the Addison

situation in forever. She had moved away during the summer before fifth grade, which definitely helped when it came to ignoring what had happened. "Do you still think of her?" Lucy asked.

"Not much," I told her. "Well, until recently."

DAY 60

"What made you think of Addison again?" Lucy asked carefully as we waited in social studies for the three o'clock bell to ring.

Part of me wanted to tell her everything: How Essie had come, and the way she looked at me—like I was Superperson—had opened an inner doorway (a magical doorway!) that led to so many paths. And how one path led to new things like woodworking and stage combat, and another path led to all the other awesome things that probably existed out there in the world, and on and on. But also, how one of the paths led backward, to fourth grade. To Rumble Peak and Addison. And I still hadn't figured out why.

But there was no way to say that to Lucy without sounding like a freak. So I just shrugged. "I'm not sure," I lied. Well, partly lied.

The bell rang, and Savannah and Essie joined us at

my locker. "I think we're set for Halloween on Saturday," Savannah announced.

"I promised my dad I'd go out for dinner with him first," Essie told us. "Apparently we're still trying to eat as much Indian food as possible."

"So, Luciana and Ollie, come at six. We'll have pizza and wait for Essie to be released from her daddy-daughter-dinner-date."

"Perfect," Lucy and I told her. But actually, I was feeling like a terrible person. For years, Annabella and I had spent Halloween together trick-or-treating. We alternated each year between superheroes and Star Wars costumes. It was supposed to be a Star Wars year, and I hadn't told them yet that I'd be ditching them to hang out with Lucy and Savannah. And Essie.

DAY 61

"So . . . ," I said nervously to Annabella when they came down to the basement for a work break and to check out my blob of wood, which was slowly becoming sort of a butterfly-hands-ish blob, "how much would you hate me if I ditched you for Halloween this year?"

Annabella stumbled and turned to Damien. "Dame? Help me pull this knife from my heart?"

I smiled. "You should take a stage combat class," I told them. "That wasn't bad."

"Thanks," they said, straightening up and smiling. "So you're doing something else this year, huh?"

I shrugged. "Maybe?"

They sighed. "Fine. I guess I'll have to act like a regular adult and hand out candy with this joker," they said, nudging Damien, who was sanding down the fruit bowl he'd been working on forever.

"Sounds torturous," he teased.

I knew Annabella was joking around about being upset, but I still felt bad. Halloween had always been our thing. I thought back to my costumes from each year since we'd begun our Halloween tradition. I'd started out as Spider-Man because, back then, I'd been less creative. The next year, we had dressed as Star Wars characters so, obviously, I was Luke. Then Peter Quill. Then young-Anakin, before he became evil. Obviously. Then Groot. Chewbacca. This year I'd been planning to recycle Groot but then Essie had arrived.

There was something about Halloween that Annabella *got*. Being anonymous leveled the playing field. Like, it partially removed gender from the equation. Not that I had any insecurity about my gender, but on Halloween anyone could be anyone, so *everyone's* gender mattered just a little bit less.

DAY 62

I had to admit to myself that *not* celebrating Halloween with Annabella and, instead, hanging out with Lucy and Savannah (and Essie, if she'd ever finish dinner with her dad and actually get to Savannah's), was a million times better than blending in with hundreds of other costume-clad humans lurking around outside in the dark.

"How is it possible that things between you and Essie could still be weird?" Savannah asked me as she and Lucy and I sat together on Savannah's kitchen island, the tray of peanut butter chip rice crispy treats that we'd just finished making at our side. The doorbell rang. Again. It was most likely trick-or-treaters, not Essie, so none of us protested when Lindsay, Savannah's little sister, ran to answer it.

"Trick-or-treat!" shouted a mass of high school–age kids who were definitely too old to be begging for candy, which made me think of myself and Annabella, who was definitely, *definitely* too old to be begging for candy.

"I have no idea how things are still weird," I told Savannah and Lucy truthfully.

"And what *I* have no idea about is why it's so difficult to *ask her* what's going on," Lucy said in that totally logical way of hers.

"Yeah, that makes *too much* sense," I joked.

She rolled her eyes and nudged me as the doorbell rang again and Savannah hopped down this time to get it. "She'll be leaving soon," Lucy reminded me. "If there's some easy way around this weirdness that you're too much of a wimp to find, you'll never forgive yourself."

I nodded noncommittally, so she nudged me again. "I wouldn't be saying this if it weren't totally obvious that she loves you, too."

DAY 64

She loves you, too.

I mean, Lucy and Savannah were pretty much always right about things, and it was true that it *seemed* like Essie still liked me. Like, *really* liked me.

She and I had been sitting on Savannah's kitchen island together, arms touching, when Savannah and Lucy had hopped down for a photo shoot with Lindsay and Savannah's dad. The energy where our arms met was like two lightsabers connecting, but obviously not in battle—in the *opposite* of battle. Essie's long hair had been hanging down the side of my arm, and all of it had brought me right back to Annabella's hammock in September: the moon, the twinkling feeling where our arms had touched, her head resting against mine.

Now we were sitting around our dining room table—me, Mom and Dad, Essie and Walter. Essie seemed . . . on edge.

Lucy would say to just ask her if she was okay, but that was obviously impossible.

I took a bite of Mom's famous cornbread (you totally couldn't even taste the quinoa flour in it) and nudged Essie, trying to cheer her up. "Hey," I said, "a smile?" I turned it over. "Or a bridge?"

Her face calmed, like she was grateful for the diversion. I wanted to put my hand on hers the way Mom or Dad would do for each other; I wanted to ask her what she was thinking about.

She seemed to relax a little into her normal, perfect self, until Walter told Mom and Dad that he'd emailed the seventh-grade teachers about Essie missing the Friday before our already-way-too-long Thanksgiving break. Wait, was he serious? I mean, if Essie went home on the Friday before break, *ten* days would pass without us seeing each other, which was an entire day more than nine days, which was already an eternity. I felt . . . deflated. And anxious, actually. Because, I realized, obsessing over Essie when she was close by was one thing. Obsessing about her when she was all the way in Saint Louis would be a different thing entirely.

DAY 65

Since Lucy and Savannah would have told me to go for it, even though it was probably too early for Essie to be up, I breathed in for four, held it for seven, exhaled for eight, and texted her: *Hey Es.*

An hour or so later (not that I was watching my phone obsessively for the three little dots), she texted back: *Hey Ol.*

Ollie   **Essie**

Sorry parents suck so bad.
Why don't u want to go
home?

I don't know how to
explain it

I get that. Like there
aren't the right words or
enough words

                              Yeah exactly

Do u want to talk about it?

                              Eh not really

Ok want me to distract u
with something?

                              Yes!

What do you think of
a poster contest for GLOW
and the winner gets their
entry blown up to poster
size and copied and passed
out to participants at the
march. Ms Rose will b the
judge. Deadline in like a
week or 2

                              Sweet!

☺ Did u finish that stupid
English essay last night

                              I wish

Are you doing anything
tonight

                              Finishing that stupid
                              English essay

Same

Want to work on it
together?

Definitely!

Cool. Ur house ok?

Sure

DAY 66

Damien peered over my shoulder to examine my progress on the butterfly-hands. Personally, I thought it was coming along nicely. As I'd been working, I'd been thinking about Essie: editing the information about the march and doing homework with her the night before; sitting next to her on my bed; the electromagnetic pulses (that I was pretty sure were coming from both me *and* her) meeting between us, turning the red and blue electricity into purple flames. Her long, wavy hair; perfect, tiny freckles; the way she locked her eyes on mine and didn't turn them away.

"Hey, if you use that narrower chisel, you'll be able to get a better line between the fingers," Damien suggested, bringing me back to his and Annabella's basement.

"Cool," I said, swapping chisels.

Damien was right; the narrower chisel was way better. I

carefully slid the blade between the fingers, peeling out thin curls of wood.

Back home, I sat at the kitchen table and watched Mom stir something on the stove. "Hey, Mom?" I asked. "What do you think of this: A poster contest for the Thankful for Pride event? The winner's art will become our logo and be blown up and displayed on all the signs at the march."

"Huh," Mom said thoughtfully. "I'm just wondering: GLOW is such an inclusive group. Does it have to be a contest? How about something a little less exclusive?"

I thought Mom's comment was dumb. If it were last year, I would have listened to her anyway. But now, at least when it came to this contest, I didn't feel like it. Why did I ask her opinion, anyway? Maybe it was just habit. I rolled my eyes at her back. "Sure, I'll think about that," I told her, knowing that I wouldn't.

DAY 67

Ollie

Lucy

Hey Lucy

Hi!!!!!!!!

If essie loves me so much
why doesn't she EVER
invite me to her house like I
literally haven't been there
since she first got here.
It is rly weird

Yeah I admit that is weird

Ask her?

Are u crazy no way that would
make me look super stalkerish

Not rly but whatev

Oh I forgot to tell u that a few
days ago I ran the poster
contest idea by ms rose &
she loves it & she had
another idea—she will pick
a winner and have posters
made and winner will find out
they won AT THE MARCH

Awesome!!!!!!

DAY 68

"Why does it have to get dark so early?" I moaned as Mom pulled out of the driveway. "It's not even five thirty. This is so depressing." My phone buzzed. I checked it quickly, hoping it would be Essie, but it was just a picture from Savannah of her and Lucy at volleyball.

"It's the worst," Mom agreed, heading toward the grocery store. "Anything new at school?"

"Nah, the usual."

"You still liking stage combat?"

"It's amazing," I told her, thinking of the special bruise-making makeup Ms. Wigg had shown us the day before.

"It's not interfering with GLOW, is it?" Mom went on.

"Mom—" I started, annoyed. She glanced at me, and in the intensity of her fake calm look, I saw years of her anxiety about whether being nonbinary was going to make life extra challenging for me. I knew she just wanted me to be okay.

Better than okay. She wanted me to be confident and happy. But I didn't feel like explaining to her that if *Essie* understood that I could juggle everything, couldn't she? "No, it's all fine."

She nodded. "Hey, you never told me what you ended up doing about the contest idea."

"What do you mean?" I asked.

"For the Thankful for Pride event."

"Yeah, we're doing it. Ms. Rose thinks it'll be great."

"Huh, I thought you were considering not doing a contest because it's so exclusive?"

"I think that was you, Mom."

"Maybe you're right," she said, turning into a parking spot at the store.

"I'm definitely right."

DAY 69

I sat at the dining room table, picking at my lentil salad (really, Mom? *Lentil salad?*), watching Mom and Dad. He poured her more water; she picked a lentil off his shirt collar (really, Dad?). I tried to remember: What had life been like before I'd come out as nonbinary, back when I hadn't minded being labeled a "girl who likes boy things"? Before Mom and Dad had become so *involved*? Max had been home, so things were louder. *Good* louder. Lucy had been my BFF. Obviously. There had been less thinking about gender. More *being*.

I helped Mom and Dad clear the table when we finished eating, and went to my room to do homework and email Ms. Rose about the T-shirts that GLOW had decided on for the march, but I couldn't focus. I turned off my lights to see if my glow-in-the-dark solar system had collected enough energy in the past few minutes to shine, which it hadn't.

So I turned the lights back on, still wondering: What had life been like before? And, had everything changed because I'd come out? I opened my laptop. Googled *Rumble Peak Amusement Park*. My fingers just moved, typing the words into the search bar like they were on a Ouija board.

I clicked over to images: The Ogre, Fortifly. And the gentler attractions. The ones a wimpy fourth grader might go on: the merry-go-round; the giant net—a house-size hammock—dotted with happy, climbing kids. It was like a part of my brain was actually trying to force me back there. To Addison Miller. To that day at the beginning of fourth grade.

I shut the computer and leaned back on my pillows.

Why was I doing this to myself?

DAY 71

Essie was waiting for me at my locker after school. "Hey, Ollie," she said in that way of hers, her eyes glued to mine, like I was the only person in the entire world.

"Hey, Essie." She had this one strand of hair that was hanging kind of crookedly over her forehead. Man, I wanted to reach out and move it. Tuck it behind her ear for her. Keep my hand there, on the side of her face.

It seemed like she was trying to get up the courage to say something. "What's up?" I asked her, hoping she'd interpret my words in their translated form: *You can tell me anything.*

"Nothing much," she replied, her eyes still on mine. Was she sending *me* a secret message? Was it the same as my secret message to her? If it was, if I *could* tell her anything, what would it be?

It would be the story of what happened at Rumble Peak, in fourth grade.

I still felt like I'd messed up back then; I'd been too-much-Ollie. Impulsive, overly trusting. Stupid. Whatever. Annabella had spent months telling me how universal my "mistake" had been.

I wanted Essie to think I was perfect, and I also wanted to tell her what had happened. But I couldn't. I didn't have the right words. "Want to come over and do homework? I'll teach you the secret rice crispy treat recipe." I wiggled my eyebrows.

She laughed. "Yeah," she said. "That sounds perfect."

DAY 76

It had been raining for days. I found a mostly broken turquoise umbrella in the black hole, aka the front closet. "Bye, Dad!" I called over my shoulder.

"Later, dude," he said from the couch. "Send Lucy my regards!"

I stepped over puddles as I tried to approximate how many times I'd walked this route to Luciana's house in my lifetime. She and I had met in kindergarten and immediately become best friends. I'd walked to her house at least once a week since then, at first with Mom, Dad, or Max; eventually on my own. What was six and a half years times fifty-two?

"Hey," I said when Lucy opened her front door and took my umbrella, "something popped into my mind as I got to your driveway. Remember roofball?"

"Random," she said. "Obviously." Lucy's house had an

awning that was perfect for the game we'd played constantly in third grade. "Minus ten for gutter balls, remember?"

"Right! We should play again," I suggested.

She looked at me like I had two heads. "Yeah. Sure. Maybe when the rain stops. Hey, want to borrow one of Diego's sweatshirts?" she asked me, eying my damp fleece.

"Maybe?" I said, laughing.

We sat on the couch and turned on the TV. I kept thinking about roofball. Luciana was crazy smart; loyal; a chess master . . . But coordinated? Not so much. Back in third grade, the girl couldn't catch a ball to save her life until we (okay, *I*) invented roofball as a way to teach her how. I was always teaching Lucy things back when we were little—how to tie her shoes, how to make friendship bracelets. In kindergarten, I actually taught her how to blow her nose.

But then in fourth grade, everything just . . . shifted. She became the one in charge, the one taking care of *me*.

DAY 78

It was weird how drastically my relationship with Lucy had changed in fourth grade, and it was also weird that it had basically taken me three years—and, maybe, Essie's arrival—to see the big picture.

The big picture was kind of like realizing that the butterfly and hands were actually the same object—something that I'd had to remind Annabella and Damien of the night before when they'd gotten into a fake fight about what my almost-finished butterfly-hands *really* was. *It's a butterfly*, Annabella had said, squinting at it.

Hands, Damien had quickly countered.

It's actually both, dummies, I'd told them. *That's the point.*

They'd looked at me, impressed, like I was some kind of brilliant philosopher.

After school, I hopped up on the stage and dug through Ms. Wigg's bin of props. She had restocked the blood capsules, which for *some strange reason* (sarcasm) had disappeared really quickly.

"Here," Franco, an eighth grader, said, handing me a "blood-soaked" bandana. "Tie this around your head." He added a stage-makeup cut to my cheekbone. I looked in the mirror. *Awesome*, I thought.

"Bewilder your audience!" Ms. Wigg reminded us (again) as we "beat each other up" on the stage. I swung my fist into Franco's face and then gut. He doubled over before spitting out a mouthful of fake, bloody teeth.

Was this heaven?

DAY 81

My phone buzzed. *Have a good T-Giving Superperson*, Essie had texted. I couldn't believe this perfect human being, who was so sure that I could do anything, was leaving me for ten days. I thought about Lucy's advice: *Just tell her what you're feeling*.

I'll miss you so much, I typed.

Then deleted it.

I want to tell you about when I was in 4th grade & I came out as nonbinary even tho it's not even a good story lol, I wrote and deleted that, too.

Essie wouldn't think that what had happened at Rumble Peak was a huge deal. She definitely wouldn't think that I had done anything wrong. And I hadn't—I *knew* that.

I flopped onto my bed. Finally, I didn't force out the memories.

Addison and I had been climbing around on the giant

hammock-net while some of our less wimpy friends, like Lucy, had gone on the roller coasters. The hammock had been swaying and rocking in a way that was just the right amount of scary. Addison, who'd had a streak of chocolate ice cream in her long blond hair, had climbed to the highest point on the net.

She'd called my name—the name that totally didn't fit me, that I used to go by. I'd glanced up at her, contemplating the climb. "Get up here, girl!" she'd encouraged.

And even though prior to that day, I'd been okay with a "girl who likes boy things" label, there was something about the way that Addison said *girl* in that moment that made me positive that it didn't fit. I'd made my way up to where she was waiting.

"I'm not a girl," I'd told her when I'd gotten to the top, all of Rumble Peak spread beneath us. "Call me Ollie, 'kay?" It was no big deal; Max had given me the nickname when I was a baby, and my family had been using it for years.

"Okay," she'd said, studying my face. It had felt like a relief, telling her. But once we'd climbed down, she'd run straight to Charlotte and Mia—two girls I'd been avoiding for the past three years—to tell them what I'd said.

The fallout was typical. Lots of looks from my classmates; too many questions from kids who had never had questions for me before that day; the teachers intervening, looking at one another like they didn't know how to talk to me about what I'd said. I hadn't understood what the big deal was. Annabella, who I hung out with all the time, had been born with what most people thought of as a "girl's body," but *they* weren't a girl. When Lucy had found me, she'd wrapped her arm around me. I can still remember standing with her, looking up through the giant net, to the sky.

I'd come home from Rumble Peak crying.

"Everyone's got a story of being outed, Ol," Annabella had said, stroking my short hair, when Mom and I had gone to their house and told them the story. "Welcome to the club."

DAY 88

Ollie

Max

Happy turkey day maximus!

> Thx best sibling in the world! U 2!

Are you at Alan's yet? BTW did you know that I only remember you're my half brother when you go to Alans for a holiday

> Haha! I forget about him a lot of the time too ;)
> Just got here

Tell him hi!

> I will! What's the word over there

I'm hiding in my room so
mom and dad wont make
me chop veggies or like
soak lentils or something

Or harvest quinoa?

Totally

Are u having tofurkey?

Anythings possible
Wish u were here!

Me too but excited to see
u next month!

♥

DAY 92

I avoided the puddles dotting the sidewalks as I rushed to school. I couldn't wait to see Essie. Ten days apart had been almost unbearable, which made it unavoidable to focus on what I'd been *trying* to ignore for months: In three weeks, she'd be gone.

When she'd been away, I'd started to worry that the distance between us might have somehow broken our bond or snuffed out our electromagnetic charge, and I needed to see her to confirm that we were still cosmically connected.

Up ahead, I spotted her purple fleece and long, blowing hair. She was sitting on the stone steps, backpack on her lap, like she was waiting for someone. I approached her, and a huge smile spread across her face. She stood up. She *was* waiting for someone. *Me.*

The frame of the open doorway inside of me caught fire. I wanted to hold her hand. "Hey," I said, instead.

"Hey!"

"How was home?" Saying that word—*home*—made me feel like crying. I wanted *this* to be Essie's home.

She shrugged, studying my eyes. "It was . . . weird."

I nodded. "Yeah."

"My parents are getting divorced. My dad is staying here next semester."

I didn't know what to say. I mean, I knew what I wanted to say: *I want you to tell me everything you're feeling.* But putting myself out there like that was obviously impossible. So I told her, "I'm really sorry. That totally sucks."

DAY 93

It was December 1, so I'd spent my entire day in a panic. Not because the march was just a few days away, but because it was officially the month that Essie was leaving. There was suddenly so much that I cared about, when last year it had just been GLOW.

Mom passed the salad. "Have you eaten any vegetables today?" she asked, smiling at me.

"Do potato chips count?"

"Definitely," Dad said.

Mom laughed. "So tell us everything that's happening with GLOW. Is there anything I can do to help with the march?"

"No, I've got this, Mom," I quickly replied.

She and Dad exchanged a look. But it was true: I was totally set. Ms. Rose and I had made our final checklist after school and everything was in place. I imagined myself walking behind the decorated Pride float, next to Essie. In my daydream, we were holding hands. "You know," I said, poking at a tomato with my fork, "you guys don't have to come to the march if you don't want to."

"Don't be silly!" Mom said. "You've put so much into this. How could we possibly miss it?"

Dad looked from her to me. "Ol, the Sociology Department *is* sponsoring the event, remember?" he said.

"Yeah, that's true."

He reached over and rubbed my hair. "We're so incredibly impressed with you. Through this event, you're doing so much for so many people. You know that, right?"

I smiled and nodded, because I did.

DAY 95

I found Ms. Wigg behind the auditorium curtain after school, digging through a bin of costumes. Zoey, Franco, and a few others were already on stage drizzling "blood" onto rags.

"Hey, Ms. Wigg," I said. "I can only stay for about fifteen minutes today. We have an after-school GLOW Club meeting," I explained.

"Oh, right! The march is tomorrow! I'll be there."

"Sweet," I said.

"Hey, can you gather the troops? I want to talk to you guys about the spring performance."

I sat on the stage between Zoey and a new seventh grader named Avi as Ms. Wigg promised everyone that they could return to soaking cloths with fake guts in just a few minutes.

"After winter vacation, we'll start prepping for the April performance," she explained. "We'll break into small groups and write our own skits that incorporate stage combat. The show will consist of a series of mini-plays."

"That sounds so sweet," Zoey whispered.

I agreed.

"We'll need to make some scheduling changes, though," Ms. Wigg went on. "A once-a-week meeting won't leave us enough prep time. So starting in January, we'll meet until four thirty on a rotating schedule, three days a week."

Three days a week? That would definitely interfere with at least some of my weekly after-school GLOW meetings and private meetings with Ms. Rose. Ms. Wigg continued talking, but I didn't pay attention to what she was saying. I couldn't ditch GLOW meetings. Obviously. I was the president of the club.

But a stage combat performance? How could I pass that up?

By the time I got to the gym, it was already bustling. I tried to push the scheduling conflict out of my mind. Maria's family had towed their flatbed trailer to the side yard earlier that day and parked it right next to the outside door for easy access. The T-shirts were on a table, ready to be passed out. It was an amazing scene.

We split up into pairs and got to work decorating the float. Essie and I made loops of duct tape and attached them to the backs of the posters we'd created in the months before, and Lucy and Savannah ran them out to the flatbed trailer.

At four thirty, we took a break. I smiled at Essie, who was sitting against the wall next to me, a loop of duct tape stuck to her hair.

"Hey," I said. "You have duct tape in your hair." I reached for it. Everyone else disappeared. It was just me and Essie, my hand in her hair. She smiled her perfect smile.

"Rabbit tape?" she asked, not moving.

In sixteen days, she'd be gone.

DAY 96

"Ollie," Mom called through my closed bedroom door, "can I come in?"

"Yup," I said, pulling my GLOW T-shirt over my thermal.

"What do you think?" Mom smiled as she joined me in front of my mirror in a GLOW T-shirt of her own.

I turned to her. "Where'd you get that?"

"Ms. Rose brought a few to my office yesterday. For the Sociology Department. A thank-you for sponsoring the event."

I nodded. It made sense. Nothing about what Mom was telling me seemed bad, or wrong, but seeing her there, smiling so proudly, wearing the same GLOW T-shirt as me made me furious.

"You okay, hon?" Mom asked.

"Yeah," I said, checking the time. "I'm fine. I'm going to meet Ms. Rose on campus to make sure the float is good to go. That way we'll have an hour if there's any last-minute stuff to do."

"Great! Dad will be home any minute and we'll come straight to campus to meet you."

"Mom, you can get there at six. I've got this."

"Ol, this is a huge deal! Dad and I are so proud. We'll be there as early as possible. We can help out if you and Ms. Rose need anything."

"Mom!" I hadn't meant to yell, and I didn't know exactly why I felt like crying, but it had something to do with the fact that Mom and Dad definitely weren't anywhere to be seen in my daydream of me and Essie at the march. I wiped my eyes. "*Please*. Come at six."

She nodded, stunned, as I pulled on my Sox cap—backward, obviously—wiped my eyes again, and walked out the door.

I crossed the street and made my way toward campus. The setting sun was low in the sky, turning the cobbled path that led to our meeting spot golden and magical-looking. Up ahead, Ms. Rose stood beside a wagon that was full of laminated signs.

"Hi, Ollie!" she called out. "Thanks for coming early!" Just behind her, our float, draped in posters and rainbow streamers, was parked on the street. "You excited?" she asked as I approached.

"Definitely!" And I was—excited for the rally, excited to see whose art was on the posters, excited to see Essie.

I picked up a cardboard sign from the wagon and looked it over. The world shifted. The two trees—Annabella's and Damien's trees, their hammock, Essie, me.

"Is this Essie's?" I asked.

Ms. Rose nodded, smiling. Of course it was. I looked around for her, feeling like someone else and exactly like myself at the same time. But Ms. Rose and I were still the only ones from GLOW on campus.

Ms. Rose darted off to reattach a streamer that had untaped itself from the float, and I sat down on a bench with the poster. The heart made of dangling branches and the curve of the hammock; Essie and me, side by side. What did it mean? I mean, did it mean what I *thought* it might mean? What was I going to say to her? My mind buzzed.

By five fifteen, most GLOW members were on campus. Lucy and Savannah were handing out posters. Joey and his Campus Press crew were setting up cameras. Even a reporter named Kiesha from ABC News was here.

But no Essie.

Mom and Dad waited until 5:45 to come, which, I guess, was impressive. For Mom. I gave them a little wave and they stayed on the periphery of the crowd, along with some other parents.

It was six o'clock. Maria's dad got into the minivan that was attached to the float and pulled out into the street.

Seven o'clock. We'd made our loop around campus, our rainbow messages illuminated by the streetlights.

By ten o'clock I was in my bed, looking up at the stars. Essie hadn't come at all.

DAY 97

The next morning, I woke up super early and sent a text to Mom and Dad (who I'd avoided *talking to* talking to the night before) so they wouldn't worry about me. Their phones chimed from the kitchen, and I left the house. Outside, I passed Annabella and Damien's and arrived at the park just as the sun was starting to break over the trees.

Standing in the sand, I spun the spinny-spin and thought about when I was little, back when being a girl was fine. There were two groups in the world as far as I knew: girl and boy. I was a girl who was like a boy. And it was cool. You need a dad for your game of "house"? *I'm in!* We're going swimming at the lake? *See ya, shirt.* You want to call me a tomboy? *Go for it.*

Something had changed in fourth grade. I'd needed a better, more accurate label. "Not a girl" had felt right, and I'd told Addison this. When I'd gotten home, Annabella had been the one who had sketched out the gender spectrum on a napkin at their kitchen table: *Girl* on the left. *Boy* on the right. A wide expanse in between. I'd always known that Annabella wasn't a woman or a man, but seeing that visual clarified something for me; as soon as I saw the area in the middle, I knew that *that* was where I fit. Specifically, just to the left of *boy*.

Being with Essie felt like those days of playing house, being the dad, swimming in my swim trunks. Because back then, gender wasn't a *thing* that I'd had to think about all the time. I just *was*.

Figuring out that my label was "nonbinary" had brought an end to those days, and that didn't seem fair, because why couldn't I be nonbinary and also *just be*? After the Rumble Peak trip, I'd had to just shrug when Ronny Francis had asked me how I could be nonbinary if the Bible said there were only girls and boys. I'd had to stand there stupidly—until Lucy had come to my rescue—when a group of girls from my class, led by Debra Marley, had surrounded me to ask me what kind of underwear I wore. And now, three years later, I had to feel bad about myself whenever I passed Ronny or Debra in the halls, even though I *knew* that I was awesome and they were losers.

And because Lucy had been the one to come to my rescue at Rumble Peak, and then so many times after that, understanding my label had also brought an end to the days when things between the two of us had felt equal.

I left the park and walked to Essie's house, where I stood

on her front porch for eight minutes until seven o'clock. Then I rang the doorbell.

After a minute, the door opened. Essie stood there, bleary-eyed, in pajama pants and a sweatshirt. I felt so mad at her for ditching me at the rally. And I felt so many other things. Seeing her made me want to cry again, and without really thinking about what I was saying, words spilled from my mouth. "You won," I told her. "How could you have just ditched me like that? Was your poster why you didn't . . . I mean, you *knew* how important the march was to me. We worked so hard on everything. How could you have just not come? I texted you, like, a thousand times. Was it because of the poster?" I asked. "It was good. Was it us? It was us, wasn't it?"

She locked her eyes on mine, and it looked like she was going to cry, too. Then she held her hand out for mine. I let her take it.

Inside, Essie led me to her inmate wall, where, in addition to way more tally marks than she'd had on it last time I'd been there, she'd drawn a massive mural. It was the poster: the hammock, the stars, the moon, our arms, held together by the magnetic force. I wondered if this was why she hadn't invited me over in months. And I wondered what else I might never know about her.

All I could say was, "In two weeks, you'll be gone."

DAY 98

"I'm sorry," Essie said for the millionth time as we lay on her carpeted floor, looking at the mural.

"I get it," I told her. "I get why you were worried about me seeing this."

"It's like Ms. VanVoorhees's optical illusions. Like you're seeing things one way, and I'm seeing the same things in a different way."

I nodded. "Yeah, like we each have our own lens."

"Ollie?" Essie asked, staring up at her mural nervously. "Was it totally obvious?"

I turned to her. "Was what obvious?" I joked. Because too-much-Ollie told me to.

She laughed. "Shut up."

"Sorry. No, just to Luciana and Savannah. They know everything, anyway. You've got guts," I went on.

"The idea to submit it to Ms. Rose just came to me. I can't believe I actually did it."

"I'm really glad that you actually did it," I said, getting up, running my hand over the mural.

"Sharpie on drywall," Essie joked, imitating Ms. VanVoorhees, who loved to give the specs of each painting she presented in class. Then she took a breath. "I ditched the rally because I couldn't bear to see your reaction. To my . . ."

"To your heart?" *Did I really just say that?*

But Essie didn't seem to mind. I lay back down next to her. "The march was everything to you," she said.

"*Part* of everything," I corrected.

"You know, I came up with this theory recently," Essie went on, "that there are different layers to everyone. You know those Russian dolls that fit one inside the other?"

"Yeah?"

"My theory is that people are like that. Like, take me, for example. My outer layer is Essie. But the smallest doll inside is *just*-Essie. The core of Essie."

"Does your core have a gender?" I wondered.

Essie thought for a second. "No," she said. "It's like . . . an essence."

"Essence of Essie?" I asked. "Wait, your core is a *perfume*?"

She laughed as I pulled up the video clip of ABC's march

coverage that Joey had forwarded to me, and rested her head against mine as I pressed *play*.

Thirteen more days.

Later that day, Mom sat down on my bed where I was "doing homework," aka thinking about Essie.

"Ol?" she said. "It's been two days. We should talk, yes?"

"Yeah, okay," I told her, closing my laptop.

"I'm sorry if I've been . . . overbearing. I want to admit something to you, which is that ever since you were little, and it became obvious that you were unique from a gender standpoint, I've been on a steadfast mission to make sure that you're confident in yourself. Gender-wise. It's possible that, as you've gotten older, I've stayed *slightly* too involved."

I tried not to smile. "Yeah," I told her. "Maybe *slightly*."

"A lot of what I've gone by was Annabella's experience. What I should say is, making your experience the *opposite* of what Annabella's was when they were a kid. Annabella has been coaching me since you were tiny, you know," she went on. "Ever since you started picking out your own clothes."

"I guess I always figured that."

"Did you? I just wanted your experience to be *drastically* drastically different from theirs. The thought of Annabella feeling like they couldn't come out until they were an adult always broke my heart."

"Mom," I said. "Can I tell you how *I* see things? Like, through *my* lens?"

She looked impressed.

"You did a good job. Like, a great job. I'm so happy with my gender-weirdness. Seriously. But I'm not *only* nonbinary. The past three years, everything has been about my gender—about making me proud and cool with it. And now that I'm thirteen? I feel like I've got this."

Mom nodded and ran her fingers through the longer part of my hair. "I know," she told me. "I believe you."

Ollie   **Lucy**

Hey lucy! What's up with Peter? Do you need any advice from the all knowing Ollie?

> Ha! Well he's only slightly aware that I exist

U should ask him to do something. Like go to jaks or something. Put yourself out there

> You sound like me lol

Lol. What else is
happening in your life

Diego passed his peanut
challenge!

Rly? That's amazing!
Should we make him
our famous rice crispy
treats???

Yes! He still has
peanut-phobia tho

We'll help him get over it

I just looked something
up. Did u know there is a
phobia called
arachibutyrophobia
which is the fear of pb
getting stuck to the roof
of ur mouth

Ur so weird

Thank you!

DAY 99

When Essie, Savannah, Lucy, and I got out of school at three o'clock, it was freezing. We'd heard murmurings all day that it was supposed to snow throughout the night, which was awesome, because in North Carolina, if it snows a centimeter, the whole state freaks out and shuts down.

Savannah pulled out her phone, screamed, and showed me, Lucy, and Essie this app she'd found that listed our "Snow Day Probability" at 82 percent.

"It's starting!" Essie said, looking up at big, wet flakes that were beginning to drop from the sky. We all shrieked and ran to my house. By the time we arrived, there was a thin coating of slushy snow on the lawn.

"I'll start the stockpile of snowballs!" Savannah announced, rolling a pea-size ball of wet snow between her fingers, laughing.

"Let me help you!" Lucy told her, and the two of them started a pile of melty snow-pebbles on the front steps.

"Come here," Essie said to me, her magnet-arm pulling toward my magnet-arm. She took my hand. We clicked together and she led me to the indentation in the lawn where slightly more snow had accumulated. "Make a snow angel with me."

DAY 100

Sure enough, I woke up the next morning to a text, voice-mail, and email from school, all announcing that we had a snow day. A thin layer of ice covered the street, and according to the news, two inches of wet snow was blanketing the grass. I texted Essie.

Ollie   **Essie**

Come over later?

                              I didn't bring my snow
                              shoes to N.C.

Haha!

                              1:00?

C u then.

I wandered out to the living room, opened Froggy's cage, and lifted her into my lap. She twitched her nose as I fed her some alfalfa. I felt bad about all the time I'd spent wishing she were a dog. It wasn't her fault that she brought up all kinds of bad memories. And hanging out in this little cage for so many hours each day? That had to suck.

An idea came to me and I texted Damien, whose classes at the university had been canceled, too. Half an hour later, I braved the tundra between our houses and met him down in his basement.

"This doesn't look hard," he confirmed, scrolling through the plans for the rabbit hutch that I'd found on my phone.

I leaned over his arm. "How are we supposed to attach this chicken wire?" I asked.

"Scroll down," he demanded.

"Yes, sir. Oh, here we go. Anyway, why is chicken wire called chicken wire? Why not rooster wire? Hey! I just got the best idea."

"Deep breaths? Yoga?" he joked.

"No! So since my butterfly-hands is coming along nicely, and since it totally sucks that I can't do stage combat next semester, and it's basically the coolest thing in the world, *and* there are so many weapons that Ms. Wigg doesn't have, you and I could make some new weapons for Stage Combat Club!"

"All right, I have to admit," Damien said, "*that* would be awesome!"

"Right? I'll research it. We could do shields, swords, daggers . . ."

"Polearms!" he added. "Maces! Axes! Flails! Wait, you did say *we*, right?'"

I wiggled my eyebrows at him.

"I'm so in," he said. "If I get fired from my teaching position for being unprepared for my classes, I'll blame it on you. Wait—" He cut himself off. "Why can't you do stage combat anymore?"

"No time," I told him, looking down at my shoes. "GLOW Club meetings."

By one o'clock, when I went home to meet Essie, I had a callus on my palm from sawing and splinters in my thumb. I liked my "new" hands: proof I was *doing* things, creating things. Things that were all mine.

I waited for her on the front steps. The snow was already starting to melt, but I managed to make one miniature snowball to hide on the porch before she arrived. By the time she walked up the front path, it was turning to a pile of slush. I held it out to her. "I was going to throw this at you," I admitted as it dripped between my fingers.

"North Carolina is so pathetic," she said, scooping up a handful of slush and tossing it at me.

I was just about to get her back when Annabella and Damien came out their front door. I waved at them.

"Is it safe to venture out?" Annabella joked, kicking a clump of slushy snow off their front steps.

"Use extreme caution," I warned. Then I turned to Essie. "I haven't introduced you to Annabella and Damien yet, have I?"

"Nope," she said.

"Let's go say 'hi.' I'm Annabella's mini me. Annabella is nonbinary, pan . . ." Essie looked confused. "It means you could be attracted to anyone on the gender spectrum."

And the look on her face when I said that? *Total relief.* Which got me thinking about the fact that I'd never put myself into Essie's shoes in *that* way. I mean, being aware of all the labels? That was old news for me. But for Essie? It was clearly *news*.

DAY 101

Ollie

Max-a-billion!

> Ol Doll! How's your
> girlfriend?

I would def not call her my
girlfriend ALSO r u asking for
mom or you?

> I promised I wouldn't talk
> to her about it

Things are great but I guess
still confusing. So . . . Max?

> Ollie?

I have to ask u something

> Shoot

Have u ever kissed
someone and it didn't like
go as planned?

                  Omg is this happening?

Is WHAT happening

                  My little sibling is coming
                  to me for relationship
                  advice!!!

DUDE

                  Ok sorry trying to be cool

                  So like was it clear that
                  everyone wanted to
                  kiss before this kiss that
                  didn't go as planned
                  happened?

It was obvious. Until it wasn't.

                  Did u ask her about it?
                  Like did you ask her
                  for her perspective on
                  things

Like the duck and rabbit?

                  Okaaay?

It seems too awkward to ask
a question like that

                  I get that but it's
                  important to talk about
                  these things so will you

promise me you'll think
about it?

I have to go, uh, wash my hair
now

Ollie?!

Ok. I'll think about it. Promise.

OK good. Keep me
posted?

Xo

That night, Dad, Essie, and I went to Satter's Platters for dinner. Despite the fact that I totally loved Dad, I kind of wished he weren't there; I wanted to be alone with Essie. I still had so many things to say to her, and in ten days she'd be back in Saint Louis. The thought made me feel nauseous.

"Lady and gentlemen, your menus," our waiter said, clearly mistaking me for a boy. Like that, for example. I wanted to talk to her about being misgendered most of the time that I wasn't at home or school, usually depending upon whether I was wearing a loose-fitting sweatshirt. I wanted to talk to her about how I used to like it, but now I wasn't so sure. But I also *didn't* want to talk to her about that, because I wanted to talk to her about *her*.

We ordered root beer, chips, and guac to start. And even though it turned out that Essie *just didn't understand* guacamole, I still loved her.

Just like when I'd put myself into Essie's shoes and felt how she might have been feeling when she heard the definition of *pan*, I put myself into her shoes and realized just how much it must suck for your parents to get divorced.

And then I thought about Max.

Ollie	Max

Hey Maximus. So you know how I always forget that you're technically my half brother unless ur at Alan's for a holiday or something. What's it like to have divorced parents

Wait who is this

Haha shut up

> Geez, O. Well . . . I can
> tell you what it's like
> for me

Ok!

> It isn't bad for me. I don't
> remember anything
> different. I mean, I call
> dad dad!

> Our dad I mean. It's prob
> more traumatic for most
> people since I was so
> young when mom and
> Alan got divorced. I only
> have memories of her
> and dad. I mean I think
> my earliest memory is
> when u were born!

Is it stressful to see Alan?

> I just feel like he's kind of
> a stranger.

> Like an uncle or
> something. He doesn't
> feel like an actual DAD

Do you like visiting him?

> I dread it but when I get
> there, it's always fine.
> Better than fine. It's fun.

Sorry I've been a crappy
sibling

                              Pardon?

Why haven't I ever asked
you about this before?

                              Because you were a
                              kid?

And now?

                              You're a teenager? Like,
                              a mature teenager who
                              seems more and more
                              adult-ish?

Sweet! OK now I'm gonna tell
u something that u seriously
can't tell mom but I want u to
know for safety purposes

                              I'm nervous

K. I need to get the glow in
the dark stickers from my
ceiling cause I wanna give
them to essie so I'm putting
my desk chair up on my bed
to reach them SO if I don't
text u back in a minute and
tell u I'm still alive and haven't
cracked my head open I want
u to call 911 K?

Waiting nervously

Waiting

I've dialed a 9

and the first 1

I'm alive!

Sweet. Well done. C u in
a week!

Can't wait!

DAY 103

When I got home from school on Friday, I spent a good while evaluating the back shed. Finally gathering enough courage to face the potential critters, I counted to three, opened the door, and ventured inside, where I pulled on the overhead bulb and dug around for the baseballs and gloves. Dad's and mine.

Once I found them, buried in a crate beneath a bunch of dirty old tennis balls, I poked my head into the kitchen, where Dad was checking on something in the slow cooker that smelled way too healthy to be edible. "Hey, Dad," I said. "Want to play catch?"

He looked over. "Really?"

"Here—" I tossed him his glove. "I even wiped off the spiderwebs."

"*You* went into the shed to get this? All by yourself?" he teased, snapping the top back onto the . . . I squinted at the open cookbook . . . black bean and kale stew? *Really, Dad?*

"Shut up," I joked. "I'm *brave*. Though I did make sure to leave the door open for a bit before going in. You know, to give the critters a chance to make a run for it."

"Wow. I barely recognize you."

Out in the yard, Dad and I assumed our regular positions. Okay, the positions that *used to be* our regular positions, back when we'd toss the ball around every day. My hand felt bigger, the glove felt smaller, but playing catch with Dad was the same: talking while tossing a ball didn't count as "talking."

"You seem happy," Dad said, launching a pop-up.

I caught it, easy. "I *feel* happy. I feel like me." I threw him a grounder.

"I'm so glad. I mean, the past couple of years must have been really stressful for you, right?" Another pop-up. "You seem more like—"

"All of me?" I asked, catching it.

"Okaaay . . . ," Dad replied as he caught my pop-up, "Sure, I can see that: all of you."

DAY 104

The rabbit hutch was done, and Essie was on her way over to see it. There was no time like the present to temporarily transport Froggy to her larger, outdoor jail.

"Here's your new vacation home, Froggy," I told her, setting her down on the grass inside the hutch. "It's nice in here, see? There are weeds to nibble on, and you can move around more . . ." I went back in for a pile of alfalfa and then sat on the back step, watching her acclimate to her new jail cell. I mean, hutch.

Froggy was cute, and I was tired of her bringing up bad memories. After Rumble Peak, I'd been embarrassed. Not by who I was. I'd *never* be embarrassed by that, unless the definition of *embarrassed* is proud. But I'd been embarrassed that I'd told Addison without really knowing if she was trustworthy, that I'd let her play such a big part. I was *still embarrassed*. For days after the incident, I'd refused to leave the house. I wouldn't go to school. I wouldn't go *anywhere*. Mom and Dad had finally bribed me with a bunny to rejoin society.

It wasn't that I had wanted the coming-out story to be some big thing, but that story? It should have been *mine*. Not Addison's.

"Ollie?" Mom called through the open window. "Essie's here!"

Essie waved, hopped down the steps, her long hair falling over her shoulders, and I smiled at her. Because *this* story—the story about me and Essie—*was* mine. I'd let Addison steal my coming-out story, but I wanted to own *everything* about the Ollie and Essie Love Story. Well, at least everything about *my* half of it.

"Hey," Essie said, sitting next to me. "Nice hutch."

"Thanks," I said. "I've been thinking . . ."

She turned to me. Our magnet bodies were so close.

"I kind of want to tell you a story. It's about when I got Froggy," I said. "No, wait. Actually, it's about me."

DAY 105

It was a warm day, especially for December. Essie and I sat on the swings, side by side, at the park. "Luciana and I used to fight over that orange swing," I told her, motioning toward the one she was on.

"You did?"

I laughed. "All the time."

"Tell me more," she said. "About when you were little."

"I was never self-conscious. I'm not talking about gender. Just in general. Until fourth grade. Then I was."

"Because of Addison?"

"Maybe. I think the whole situation just derailed me."

She nodded.

I went on. "I always wanted to be the best at whatever I was doing, even if it was something totally dumb. I got so mad once in second grade, because this kid collected a bigger pile of pebbles than me at recess."

"*Jerk*," Essie confirmed.

"I broke my arm in third grade falling out of a tree."

"Yikes."

"I was kind of proud of the cast, actually. Now tell me about you. What were *you* like when you were little?"

"My best friend was Emily."

"And?"

"I went through a phase where I'd only eat foods that were primary colors."

"Of course," I joked.

"I used to be obsessed with horses. And I had a fuzzy collection."

"A fuzzy collection?"

"Yeah. Anytime I'd find something fuzzy, like a piece of lint on the rug, I'd put it in a jar."

I laughed as Essie jumped off her swing. "Didn't you tell me before that Damien was expecting you at five?" she asked, tapping her watch.

"Yeah." I'd told him I'd be over to work on my stage weapons. I wanted to go, but I didn't want to go. "Come with?" I asked her.

"Damien?" I called through his and Annabella's screen door when Essie and I arrived. "You there?"

"Come in!" he yelled from downstairs.

"Follow me," I told Essie, leading her down to the basement.

"Hey, Ollie! Oh, you brought Essie!" Damien said, drill in hand.

"Do you have time for another student?"

"There's a waiting list, but if the student is Essie Rosenberg, she can jump the queue."

"Great!" I said.

"Does my new student have a project idea in mind? No more rabbit hutches, I hope."

"I was actually hoping to build a duck pond," Essie replied, giggling.

Damien looked worried. I cracked up. "Relax. She's kidding. She's going to help me make stage weapons."

"I am?" she asked.

"You are. Making them is my concession prize for dropping out of stage combat."

"Wait, what?" she asked. "Why are you dropping out?"

I explained how I couldn't be at GLOW meetings *and* stage combat meetings at the same time.

"Ollie," Essie said, "remember: You're Superperson. Can't you figure out some way to make it work?"

Damien pulled out a couple of saws and some sandpaper, and left us to do some work.

I thought about what Essie had said as she took a step

backward and skeptically examined the saws. So I'll admit to being a wimp about roller coasters (and anything else that moves), but I definitely wasn't afraid of Damien's tools. Essie, it turned out, was the exact opposite. Apparently, she loved all the craziest rides at amusement parks. But when I picked up the tiniest saw, she practically screamed.

"You have to chill out!" I told her when she found a pair of giant leather work gloves to wear as she sanded the dagger Damien and I had started a few days earlier.

"I'm scared of blood," she admitted, giggling.

I laughed. "You look so funny with that tiny piece of sandpaper and enormous gloves that practically go up to your shoulders!"

"Shut up, or I'll maul you with this," she said, waving the scrap of sandpaper in my face.

Essie and I got into kind of a rhythm, standing there together, sanding wood. It was nice, like the cores of who we were just-*being* together.

Eventually, Annabella called to us from upstairs. "Hey, humans," they yelled. "It's not that we don't love you, but you're getting the boot. Damien and I have a thing to go to."

"'Kay," I called up. "Cleaning up now." I swept sawdust into the dustpan that Essie held for me. "I'm proud of you," I told her. "It was really brave, how you touched the handle of that saw with the tip of your finger a couple of minutes ago."

"Shut up," she said, dumping the sawdust onto my shoes.

"Hey!" I swept up the pile—*again*—laughing.

"How's the gothic arming sword coming along?" Damien asked when we came upstairs. Annabella shoved his coat into his hands.

"Almost done," I confirmed.

"Excellent," Damien told me as Annabella hurried us all out the door. Outside, the sun was setting. Essie and I waved to Damien and Annabella as they rushed off.

"Do you have to go home?" I asked Essie.

"Not for like an hour. I have to . . . I want to FaceTime my mom when she's back from a meeting."

I nodded.

She nodded. "So . . ."

"We could sit in the hammock for a bit?"

We lay back in the netting, looking up at the darkening sky. Essie put her thumbs together. "Butterfly," she said.

I squeezed them. They were so warm. "Hands."

DAY 106

Essie and I were in the backyard on Monday after school, sitting side by side, watching Froggy do her bunny thing. In other words, lying there, sleeping. I thought of my text conversation with Max. This was my last week with Essie. My last chance to find out how things had looked all this time through her eyes. "Es?" I asked.

"Yeah?"

My heart thudded. *Just do it, Ollie!* "What made you stop liking me? You know, after the spinny-spin."

"What?" she asked, staring at me. "I never stopped liking you. *You* stopped liking *me*."

"No I didn't!" I looked from her perfect face to her hand, which was so close to mine. "Essie?"

"Yeah?"

"Can I . . ." God, this was awkward. "Can I hold your hand?"

She grabbed my hand. Wrapped her fingers through mine.

"I *never* stopped liking you," she repeated. Tiny drops of rain were starting to fall.

"It seemed like you did. I was worried that you weren't into me because I'm nonbinary." There. Simple. Not easy, but simple.

She shook her head. "No, that wasn't it. That was never it."

"So what happened? On the spinny-spin."

"Maybe I panicked?" Her eyes were so brown and her bottom eyelashes curled all the way onto her freckled skin. "I don't know," she finally admitted. "I don't know what happened."

Suddenly, it seemed kind of obvious. "Do you think maybe you were just overwhelmed, in general? Because of your parents separating, and your mom staying back in Saint Louis?"

"Maybe?" she said, looking suddenly so sad, like she was mulling over something that she'd never understand. "It's just that, before they separated, there was at least always some hope that they'd start liking each other. That we'd be the kind of family I wanted us to be. You know?"

I nodded. "It's okay," I told her. "It's okay to be sad." I reached my arm around her.

She leaned her head against mine. "Yeah."

My rabbit: Essie isn't attracted to me because I'm nonbinary. Essie's duck: I'm sad. My hands: Essie stopped inviting me over, so there you have it—proof. Essie's butterfly: My heart is on my wall.

DAY 107

It was like I was returning to the Ollie I was before—before I'd become focused *only* on my gender.

"What are you thinking about?" Essie asked, as we sat on the stone steps before school.

I held up my phone to show her my text exchange with Lucy. "Lucy and Peter have a homework date."

"It's about time!" she said.

"Yeah, I gave Lucy the advice she always gives me. Apparently she thought she had some smart ideas! Hey, I've been thinking. Do you ever wish you could go back to being young?" I thought of teaching Lucy to catch roofballs, playing baseball with Dad, the days when my brain was freer.

Essie reached for my hand, wove her fingers through mine. Smiled. "Only sometimes," she replied.

* * *

After lunch, I tossed my garbage in the trash (LeBron style) wondering if there were any coed basketball leagues in the area that I could join, because basketball was one of those things I'd given up due to the whole *gendered-sport thing*, and I really wished I could still play. Then I went to Ms. Rose's classroom. She was at her desk, her back to me. I didn't want to scare her. "Hey, Ms. Rose," I whispered.

She jumped anyway. "Ollie! You scared me!"

"Sorry. I tried not to."

She took a deep breath. "Okay. Recovered. Come in!"

I sat down at the desk nearest to hers. "Can we talk about next semester? GLOW?" I asked her.

"Of course! What's up?"

"I got an idea. What if, starting after winter break, I had a co-president? That way, I'd still be totally involved, but maybe I wouldn't have to come to every single meeting. It would give me more time to do other clubs, too."

Ms. Rose looked thoughtful. "That's a very mature idea. I really, *really* like it. How'd you come up with it?"

I shrugged, thinking of Essie. The open doorway. The way she thought I could do everything. "It just came to me."

Lucy was on the stone steps, waiting for me after school. "How are you?" she asked. "Four more days, huh?"

"I'm okay," I told her. "I'm going to be okay. Eventually."

I forced a smile. "Any Peter updates?" I asked, sending her a secret message: I'm not *just* going to look at things through my lens anymore.

She smiled, like she'd received it. "I'm meeting him at the library in an hour to do homework."

DAY 108

Essie had been obsessing. Over words. Labels. She was reminding me of *me*, in fourth grade. The bell dinged as we entered Jak's. "A word is just a word, right?" she was saying as we approached the counter.

I interrupted her. "Would it be weird for anyone other than a little kid to order Blue Moon?"

"Like that!" she said. "Why would we label ice cream flavors that way, some for kids and some for adults?"

"Right." I scanned the labels, looking for the most adult-like one. "I'll have a scoop of Mocha Chip," I told Jak. Essie ordered, and we took our ice cream outside. "I used to obsess about this, too," I assured her, taking a bite and wishing I *had* ordered Blue Moon, after all. "Labels—the benefits, the drawbacks . . ."

"And then?"

"I guess I moved on . . . started obsessing about different

things. Space, Star Wars, superheroes, Basketball. GLOW . . ."

You . . .

"Yeah . . . ," she said, licking her cone.

I started thinking of *all* of my labels—because even though my gender label was one of my favorite and most important labels, I liked thinking about the other ones, too, and I knew that without them I wouldn't be me. *White. Upper-middle class. Competitive. Athletic. Sibling. Child. Woodworker. Stage fighter. Founder of GLOW. Only and always high-top-wearer. Wannabe dog owner. President: Essie Rosenberg Fan Club.*

"I just think," Essie said, "that life should be about *things*, not the *words* for things."

"Are you talking about gender and sexuality labels, by any chance?"

"Maybe."

"My experience was that the labels didn't seem like a big deal for too long."

Essie nodded, thinking.

"Can I tell you something about my 'President of GLOW' label?" I asked, after a minute of silence.

Essie nodded. "Sure."

"I asked Ms. Rose what she thought about me having a co-president next semester."

"Really?"

"Yeah, you helped me realize that I can do lots of stuff. Like, GLOW plus other things. I can do stage combat, woodworking . . ."

"And you can text me?" she interrupted, looking kind of thoughtful, or mysterious, or something.

"Yeah," I said, "I can text you."

When we got back to Essie's, her dad was waiting for us. He'd moved her bed away from the wall and laid drop cloths down on the ugly beige carpet. "It's a great mural," he said, handing us paintbrushes. "I'll be sad to see it go." Then he opened the windows so we wouldn't suffocate on paint fumes and left the room.

For a long time, Essie and I stared at the wall; at us, in the hammock, back in September. Then I picked the glow-in-the-dark stickers off where we'd placed them, inside Essie's heart.

"At least you can put them back on your ceiling," she said.

"No, I want you to have them. For your room back home."

"Okay, but you keep the moon."

The first coat of white paint lightened the mural, like a dream that fades when you try to remember it in the morning.

With the second coat, it was gone.

DAY 109

"Maxi Pad!" I yelled, running through the front door after school.

"Ol Doll!" he screamed from the kitchen.

We ran toward each other in pretend slo-mo as Mom stood back and watched happily. Max scooped me up like a baby when we met and tossed me onto the couch. "You got tall!" he said, sitting down next to me.

"Did I?" I asked. "I'm starving *all* the time."

"Me too," he said. "Speaking of which, what's for dinner, Mom?"

"Good question," she answered. "I'm making soup. We can have that tonight or tomorrow. It's usually better when it sits for a day. Your choice, Max."

Pizza Pizza, I mouthed at him.

"I was thinking of Pizza Pizza . . . ," he said, "but I'm not sure."

I scowled.

"I mean, I unpacked all my stuff. It's in a gross pile on my bed and is going to take *forever* to put away . . ."

I kicked him. "Fine, I'll *help*," I said. "But," I went on, "in exchange for helping you clean *your* room so we can go to *your favorite restaurant, I* have a favor to ask *you*."

"Ask away!"

"Privately," I told him.

"Hey," I said to Mom's back. She was at the stove, stirring the soup.

"How are you?" she asked, pulling me next to her.

"Eh," I told her, envisioning life without Essie.

"Yeah." She seemed to *get* what I was saying.

"What kind of soup?" I asked.

"Squash."

Gross.

"Remember when we used to cook together?" I asked her suddenly. *I'd* practically forgotten about that.

"Of course! When you were in elementary school, I could always get you to talk to me if you were busy doing something else at the same time. I realized if I put you to work chopping something, you'd tell me what was on your mind."

"I did?"

She smiled. "I need some more diced garlic cloves. You game?"

At the sink, I scrubbed the remainder of white paint out from under my fingernails. Then I went to work.

Apparently, chopping stuff with Mom still made me say things I normally wouldn't because, all of a sudden, without realizing it was going to come out, I told her, "I think I should talk to Mr. Bell about the fact that I've been using the girl's locker room for long enough. I mean, I've just been changing there because it's convenient. But it doesn't make sense. I should probably see what the other options are. What we *really* need is a gender-neutral locker room."

Mom nodded. "That's true! Want me to call him and—" She cut herself off and looked at me out of the corner of her eye, smiling a little. "You've got this, right?"

"Right," I confirmed. "So," I said as she handed me another garlic clove, "what's new at work?"

"You actually want to know?" she asked. "It's totally boring."

I shrugged. "Try me."

After dinner at Pizza Pizza, Max and I drove toward Essie's to pick her up. "She still doesn't know where you're taking her?" Max asked as we turned onto her street.

"Not a clue. Thanks for the ride, Maxi Pad." I held out my hand. "Cash?" I asked, wiggling my eyebrows.

"We still haven't discussed your plan to pay me back," he said, handing me the money.

"You could think of it as an investment, of some sort," I suggested.

He smiled, stopping in front of Essie's house, honking the horn. "Nice try. Hey. I know I keep saying this, but you seem so much older all of a sudden," he told me.

"I guess it happens."

"I guess so." He tousled my hair.

Max and Essie spent the twenty-minute drive engaged in an intensive getting-to-know-you session, which consisted of him grilling her on all the Most Important Things: Favorite food? (Cheese melted on carbs.) Least-favorite food? (Avocado.) *No relationship is perfect, Ollie*, I told myself. Favorite animal? (Baby sloth.) Favorite color? (Clear.) I was starting to feel sorry for Essie because of Max's seemingly endless list of questions, but she seemed to like playing the Q&A game, which made me love her even more.

Eventually, we pulled up at the front gates of Rumble Peak. Essie and I got out of the car, and I walked around to Max's open window as she waited for me on the curb.

"Nine o'clock, right here?" he confirmed.

I nodded. "Thanks for the ride."

He looked from Essie to me. "I approve," he whispered. "There's the issue of the avocados, but we can probably work around that, right?"

I smiled. "Probably," I whispered back. Then he drove off, and I took Essie's hand.

At the far end of the park, past the roller coasters, the merry-go-round, and the endless food stands, the giant hammock hung, dirty white against the dark gray sky. And even though I was bigger than I'd been three years before, it still seemed huge and daunting. I felt Essie's eyes on me as I guided her to the rope ramp that led to the highest part of the net. All of it was exactly the same as it had been, except that everything was different now.

Essie stumbled on the netting behind me as we made our way upward. "Are you okay?" I asked her, turning around.

She wiggled her foot out of where it had caught on the net and nodded. "Are you?"

"I think so."

We climbed up the gentle incline past a bunch of little kids who were jumping around excitedly, making our way to the highest point of the hammock, where nobody else was. All I could see from that high up was the star-studded sky. Essie and sky. We lay down next to each other and I tried to ignore what was hanging over us—the fact that the next day, Essie would be gone.

"We're not here because of Addison Miller," I told her.

"Okay," she said, turning on her side, touching my cheek.

I really didn't want to cry. "I figured out—because of, like, this doorway that you opened inside of me when we met—that pretty much in this exact spot, three years ago, I split into two parts: the part of me that has to do with my gender, and the rest of me. Being with you helped me realize that I should get to be *all of me*."

"And you wanted to come back?" Essie asked. "So you could weave the parts back together?"

I nodded.

"Is it working?"

"I think so," I told her, "because I feel whole."

She smiled and my heart fluttered. "Ollie?" she said.

"Yeah?" I asked, looking at her pale face and wind-blown hair.

"So just before you and Max picked me up, my dad and I FaceTimed my mom. First off, she says hi. I told her about you."

"You did?"

"Yeah. *All* about you."

I smiled and she went on. "A few days ago, I asked them a

big question. Then they had a million hours of phone conversations and today they gave me their verdict."

I was starting to feel weird. Like, good-nervous-weird. "Okay," I said again.

"I asked my parents if I could stay with my dad for the rest of the year. *Here*. Because it didn't seem fair for them to uproot me twice in seventh grade, and why should I have to go home now? I don't *want* to go home now."

I sat up. "And?"

Essie smiled—the world's most perfect smile. "They said yes."

DAY 110

Ollie

Essie

Is the warden asleep?

If by asleep you mean drinking coffee and grading papers on the couch yes.

Can you meet me at the corner?

The moon is awesome. Let's go to A & D's hammock

Hang on a sec, let me ask

Yup!

Essie walked toward the corner—our corner—in fuzzy pajama pants and a purple hoodie. Moonlight flooded the sidewalk.

I could feel the magnetic pull; the closer Essie got, the stronger it was. When she stopped in front of me, the magnets sucked our hands together, palm to palm.

I wrapped my fingers around hers. "Essie?" I asked, suspecting I was about to sound ridiculous. "Do you ever feel like maybe we're magnets? Like those really strong ones, from science class?"

"Wait," she said, smiling, "are you talking about the zaps?"

"I guess you could call it that," I said, studying her eyes. "Like the magnets pull us together and we click and—"

"There's a zap?"

"There's a zap," I confirmed.

Hand in hand, we walked around the corner to Annabella and Damien's yard. Their hammock was bright white in the moonlight. We lay back in it and looked up at the stars. The moon was a perfect crescent. I pulled my completed butterfly-hands carving out of my sweatpants pocket. "I made you something," I told her.

"Wow," she said, holding it up. "I love it. What do you see? A butterfly? Or hands?"

"Both," I told her without hesitating. "You?"

"Definitely both."

It felt like the first time Essie and I had been in the hammock three months before, only better, because in the time between then and now, *because of her*, I'd found the parts of myself that I'd practically forgotten about for three years. They'd been waiting for me on the giant hammock at Rumble Peak, exactly where I'd left them.

I turned my head to Essie. Our faces were like magnets. Like always. "Essie?" I asked, "Can I—"

She nodded. "Definitely, yes."

Our lips touched.

Zap.

ACKNOWLEDGMENTS

I continue to be grateful beyond measure for the kind souls who support me from near and far. Kim Bell, the duck to my rabbit and butterfly to my hands, thank you for the seed that became the idea that became this book. And for all the other seeds. Wendy Schmalz, thank you for always keeping the faith. Joy Peskin, you nurtured my writing with great wisdom and heart. Thank you for taking such incredibly good care of Ollie and Essie. Elizabeth Lee, thank you for your thoughtful input and enthusiasm along the way. Caleb Hosalla, I am grateful for the beautiful cover that you created. Cassie Gonzales, Avia Perez, Nicole Wayland, and Linda Minton, thank you for all of your behind-the-scenes contributions to *Spin with Me*. Henry Alberto, Agnes Borinsky, and Rae MacCarthy, your thorough and thoughtful sensitivity reads were invaluable. Finally, Daniel, B & E, thank you for continuing to be the inspiration for everything I do.